Quotable Sherlock

Compiled & Edited by
David W. Barber

Quotable Sherlock

Compiled & Edited by
David W. Barber
Illustrations by Sidney Paget

The Quotable Press

Introduction

In Sherlock Holmes and Dr. Watson, author Sir Arthur Conan Doyle created two of the most recognizable – and memorable – characters ever invented in English literature. So well known, in fact, that many people thought at the time, and still think, Holmes and Watson were real people, and not merely fictional characters, and Doyle served only as Watson's "literary agent" to get the stories into print. It's part of the Sherlockian game to maintain this little conceit even today. (For a more complete biography of Conan Doyle, see Page 103.)

A Study in Scarlet, The Hound of the Baskervilles and others of the 56 short stories and four novels that make up the Sherlockian "Canon" first appeared in Victorian London serialized in the *Strand* magazine and others, and were later published in book form. The stories were widely read and quickly became popular, both in Britain and abroad. For more than a century since, they have delighted and intrigued readers all over the world, selling millions of copies in languages ranging from French, German and Norwegian to Japanese, Urdu and Ukrainian. (In Hebrew, lacking the initial consonant H, the hero must go by the name Golmes.)

The cerebral, emotionally distant consulting detective and his bluff but faithful narrator and sidekick were later immortalized on stage by William Gillette (and still later by Leonard Nimoy, *Star Trek*'s Mr. Spock) and on screen by Basil Rathbone (with Nigel Bruce), Christopher Plummer (with James Mason), Jeremy Brett (with Edward Hardwicke) and a wide variety of other actors. Caricatured with deerstalker on head and magnifying glass in hand, a lampooned Sherlock Holmes has also appeared in countless editorial cartoons, print and TV ads, and just about everywhere else you might imagine. (Tax accountant to deerstalkered detective: "Some of these deductions are remarkable, Mr. Holmes.") Many authors (including this one) have written pastiches or parody stories that continue the adventures beyond the boundaries Doyle first set.

Leading up to the first story (*A Study in Scarlet*, first published in *Beeton's Christmas Annual* in 1887), Doyle had considered several names for his detective hero before settling on Sherlock Holmes. Doyle took both names from men he admired – the first name from a cricket player named Thomas Sherlock, the surname from Oliver Wendell Holmes (Sr.), an American poet, novelist and doctor and the father of Oliver Wendell Holmes (Jr.), the revered judge and statesman. Among the names Doyle had rejected were Ormond Sacker, Sherringford Hope and Sherringford Holmes – thus saving fans the embarrassment of referring to themselves as "Ormondians" or "Sherringfordians."

Dr. John H. Watson was named after a medical colleague of Doyle's in Southsea, James Watson. (Hence, probably, Watson's wife's mistaken reference to him as "James" in *The Man with the Twisted Lip*, a slip that has kept scholars scrambling for years.) Holmes's nemesis, the evil Professor Moriarty, apparently gets his name from a teacher of Doyle's early schooling at Stonyhurst College. (And how many of us would also like to name villains after bad teachers in our past?)

Holmes's legendary powers of deduction and inference were at least partly inspired by Dr. Joseph Bell, an instructor of Doyle's when he studied medicine in Edinburgh, who apparently impressed on his students the need for keen observation and deductive reasoning.

Although the Great Detective is generally a serious fellow, the original stories often have both a droll sense of humor and even at times a profound insight into the human condition. Many of their phrases and expressions – "Elementary," "The plot thickens," "The game's afoot!" and others – have entered into the lexicon of everyday speech. (Well, in certain circles, anyway.)

But probably the most famous Sherlockian expression, even for those who've never even read the stories, is, of course, a line he never utters. Like the famously misquoted "Play it again, Sam" (likewise a line neither Bogart nor anyone else in *Casablanca* ever says) nowhere in the official Canon does Holmes ever actually say, "Elementary, my dear Watson." He does say "Elementary" (though less often than you might think) and he frequently says "My dear Watson," but surprisingly, he never combines them to form the now-famous line – though he really ought to have. He far more frequently says, "You know my methods, Watson," or some variation of it, though that phrase has never gained the same resonance. (The deerstalker cap and curved pipe aren't exactly Canonical either, but they've become indelibly associated with the image, thanks initially to the original illustrations by Sidney Paget, some of which are reproduced here, and later by the movies and TV shows.)

Doyle developed a distinct love/hate relationship with Holmes and Watson. As a struggling writer, he was grateful for the exposure the stories gained him (and probably even more grateful for the money they earned, which grew with their popularity and allowed him to stop practising medicine). But after two novels and 23 stories, he grew tired of writing the detective potboilers, and frustrated that they were taking attention away from what he regarded (mistakenly, as it turns out) as his better and more important works – the Professor Challenger adventures and such Sir Walter Scottish historical romances as *Sir Nigel* and *The White Company*. (Writers are not always the best judges of what the public will remember them for.) So he killed off Holmes, plunging him and Moriarty over the precipice of the Reichenbach Falls in a story aptly named *The Final Problem*.

The public outcry was enormous, so much so that Doyle was forced to bring him back, first in *The Hound of the Baskervilles* (not a full resurrection, since it's set in a time before his supposed death) and later more fully in *The Empty House*, the first story in the aptly named collection *The Return of Sherlock Holmes*. Since then, the old faked-death routine has become a staple of Hollywood movies and TV in all sorts of genres.

Doyle tried again to wind up the series in *His Last Bow*, a story set on the eve of the First World War that has Holmes and Watson coming out of retirement to thwart a couple of German spies, and with motorcars and electric lights replacing the familiar Hansom cabs and gaslamps. (In real life, Doyle gave early warnings of the threat of a submarine attack on Britain and lobbied hard for the use of lifejackets for the navy during the war.) But yet again, lured by the personal and financial recognition, he later returned to writing what the public wanted to read, the dozen adventures collected together in *The Case Book of Sherlock Holmes*.

There are problems in the stories – is Watson's name John or James? Is his Afghan war wound in the leg or the shoulder? – and some of Holmes's (that is, Doyle's) deductions are based on faulty reasoning. He can't, as he tells Watson in *The Six Napoleons*, have solved "the dreadful business of the Abernetty family" by observing "the depth which the parsley had sunk into the butter upon a hot day." Parsley won't sink into butter – the butter melts out from beneath it. (Believe me, I've tried it.) And his trick in *The Priory School* of determining which way the bicycle went based on the depth of the tire tracks not only defies the laws of physics, but also of bicycle design.

But never mind, we like the stories anyway. Although their creator may have grown weary of Holmes and Watson, a portion of the reading public never has. And even though technology has advanced and the detective genre has become more sophisticated, each generation of readers seems happy to rediscover the pleasures of a world where gaslight glows, the London fog swirls and the game is always afoot.

My thanks go to Geoff Savage of Sound And Vision Publishing and *The Quotable Press*, for his faith in, and support of, this new Quotable series.

DWB
Toronto, 2001

"Dr Watson, Mr. Sherlock Holmes."

"Dr. Watson, Mr. Sherlock Holmes."
> Stamford introducing Watson and Holmes,
> *A Study in Scarlet*, Part 1, Chap. 1

"You have been in Afghanistan, I perceive."
> Holmes to Watson, on first meeting,
> *A Study in Scarlet*, Part 1, Chap. 1

"It is always a joy to meet an American ..."

"American slang is very expressive sometimes."
> Holmes to Lord St. Simon,
> *The Noble Bachelor*

"It is always a joy to meet an American, Mr. Moulton, for I am one of those who believe that the folly of a monarch and the blundering of a minister in far-gone years will not prevent our children from being some day citizens of the same world-wide

1

country under a flag which shall be a quartering of the Union Jack with the Stars and Stripes."

Holmes to Frank Moulton,
The Noble Bachelor

"Oh, an Irish-American?"

"If you heard him talk you would not doubt it. Sometimes I assure you I can hardly understand him. He seems to have declared war on the King's English as well as on the English king."

Von Bork to Von Herling on Holmes, posing as Altamont,
His Last Bow

"Art for its own sake ..."

"Chance has put in our way a most singular and whimsical problem, and its solution is its own reward."

Holmes to Watson,
The Blue Carbuncle

On glancing over my notes of the seventy odd cases in which I have during the last eight years studied the methods of my friend Sherlock Holmes, I find many tragic, some comic, a large number merely strange, but none commonplace; for, working as he did rather for the love of his art than for the acquirement of wealth, he refused to associate himself with any investigation which did not tend towards the unusual, and even the fantastic.

Watson on Holmes,
The Speckled Band

"To the man who loves art for its own sake," remarked Sherlock Holmes, tossing aside the advertisement sheet of the *Daily Telegraph*, "it is frequently in its least important and lowliest manifestations that the keenest pleasure is to be derived."

Holmes to Watson,
The Copper Beeches

"The work itself, the pleasure of finding a field for my peculiar powers, is my highest reward."

Holmes to Watson,
The Sign of Four, Chap. 1

Holmes had the impersonal joy of the true artist in his better work, even as he mourned darkly when it fell below the high level to which he aspired.

Watson on Holmes,
The Valley of Fear, Part 1, Chap. 1

"Art in the blood is liable to take the strangest forms."

Holmes to Watson,
The Greek Interpreter

"Instead of being ruined, my good sir, you will find that your reputation has been enormously enhanced. Just make a few alterations in that report which you were writing, and they will understand how hard it is to throw dust in the eyes of Inspector Lestrade."

"And you don't want your name to appear?"

"Not at all. The work is its own reward."

Holmes and Insp. Lestrade,
The Norwood Builder

Holmes, however, like all great artists, lived for his art's sake, and, save in the case of the Duke of Holdernesse, I have seldom known him claim any large reward for his inestimable services. So unworldly was he – or so capricious – that he frequently refused his help to the powerful and wealthy where the problem made no appeal to his sympathies, while he would devote weeks of most intense application to the affairs of some humble client whose case presented those strange and dramatic qualities which appealed to his imagination and challenged his ingenuity.

Watson on Holmes,
Black Peter

"Why should you go further in it? What have you to gain from it?"

"What, indeed? It is art for art's sake, Watson. I suppose when you doctored you found yourself studying cases without thought of a fee?"

"For my education, Holmes."

"Education never ends, Watson. It is a series of lessons with the greatest for the last."

Watson and Holmes,
The Red Circle

"I play the game for the game's own sake."

Holmes to Mycroft Holmes,
The Bruce-Partington Plans

... like those of a trained bloodhound ...

"If a herd of buffaloes had passed along, there could not be a greater mess."

Holmes to Insp. Gregson,
A Study in Scarlet, Part 1, Chap. 3

"It's all very well for you to laugh, Mr. Sherlock Holmes. You may be very smart and clever, but the old hound is the best, when all is said and done."

Insp. Lestrade to Holmes,
A Study in Scarlet, Part 1, Chap. 3

As he spoke, he whipped a tape measure and a large round magnifying glass from his pocket. With these two implements he trotted noiselessly about the room, sometimes stopping, occasionally kneeling, and once lying flat upon his face. So engrossed was he with his occupation that he appeared to have forgotten our presence, for he chattered away to himself under his breath the whole time, keeping up a running fire of exclamations, groans, whistles, and little cries suggestive of encouragement and of hope. As I watched him I was irresistibly reminded of a pure-blooded, well-trained foxhound, as it dashes backward and forward through the covert, whining in its eagerness, until it comes across the lost scent.

Watson on Holmes,
A Study in Scarlet, Part 1, Chap. 3

"Our friend here is a wonderful man for starting a chase. All he wants is an old dog to help him to do the running down."

Peter Jones of Scotland Yard on Holmes,
The Red-Headed League

Sherlock Holmes was transformed when he was hot upon such a scent as this. Men who had only known the quiet thinker and logician of Baker Street would have failed to recognize him. His face flushed and darkened. His brows were drawn into two hard black lines, while his eyes shone out from beneath them with a steely glitter. His face was bent downward, his shoulders bowed, his lips compressed, and the veins stood out like whipcord in his long, sinewy neck. His nostrils seemed to dilate with a purely animal lust for the chase, and his mind was so absolutely concentrated upon the matter before him that a question or remark fell unheeded upon his ears, or, at the most, only provoked a quick, impatient snarl in reply.

Watson on Holmes,
Boscombe Valley

"Halloa! What have we here?"

Holmes,
The Second Stain

So swift, silent, and furtive were his movements, like those of a trained bloodhound picking out a scent, that I could not but think what a terrible criminal he would have made had he turned his energy and sagacity against the law instead of exerting them in its defence.

Watson on Holmes,
The Sign of Four, Chap. 6

Sherlock Holmes's eyes glistened, his pale cheeks took a warmer hue, and his whole eager face shone with an inward light when the call for work reached him

Watson on Holmes,
The Valley of Fear, Part 1, Chap. 2

His eyes shone, and his cheek was flushed with the exhilaration of the master workman who sees his work lie ready before him. A very different Holmes, this active, alert man, from the introspective and pallid dreamer of Baker Street.

Watson on Holmes,
The Priory School

His eager face still wore that expression of intense and high-strung energy, which showed me that some novel and suggestive circumstance had opened up a stimulating line of thought. See the foxhound with hanging ears and drooping tail as it lolls about the kennels, and compare it with the same hound as, with gleaming eyes and straining muscles, it runs upon a breast-high scent – such was the change in Holmes since the morning. He was a different man from the limp and lounging figure in the mouse-coloured dressing-gown who had prowled so restlessly only a few hours before round the fog-girt room.

Watson on Holmes,
The Bruce-Partington Plans

One realized the red-hot energy which underlay Holmes's phlegmatic exterior when one saw the sudden change which came over him from the moment that he entered the fatal apartment. In an instant he was tense and alert, his eyes shining, his face set, his limbs quivering with eager activity. He was out on the lawn, in through the window, round the room, and up into the bedroom, for all the world like a dashing foxhound drawing a cover.

Watson on Holmes,
The Devil's Foot

"He held an old black boot in the air."

From amid a tuft of cotton grass which bore it up out of the slime some dark thing was projecting. Holmes sank to his waist as he stepped from the path to seize it, and had we not been there to drag him out he could never have set his foot upon firm land again. He held an old black boot in the air. "Meyers, Toronto" was printed on the leather inside.

Watson,
The Hound of the Baskervilles, Chap. 5

"I am lost without my Boswell."

"I should prefer having a partner to being alone."

Watson to Stamford,
A Study in Scarlet, Part 1, Chap. 1

"Your merits should be publicly recognized. You should publish an account of the case. If you won't, I will for you."

Watson to Holmes,
A Study in Scarlet, Part 2, Chap. 7

"I am lost without my Boswell."

Holmes to Watson,
A Scandal in Bohemia

"Oh, a trusty comrade is always of use; and a chronicler still more so.

Holmes to Watson,
The Man with the Twisted Lip

"If I claim full justice for my art, it is because it is an impersonal thing – a thing beyond myself. Crime is common. Logic is rare. Therefore it is upon the logic rather than upon the crime that you should dwell. You have degraded what should have been a course of lectures into a series of tales."

Holmes to Watson,
The Copper Beeches

"I hear of Sherlock everywhere since you became his chronicler."

Mycroft Holmes to Watson,
The Greek Interpreter

"Hopkins has called me in seven times, and on each occasion his summons has been entirely justified," said Holmes. "I fancy that every one of his cases has found its way into your collection, and I must admit, Watson, that you have some power of selection, which atones for much which I deplore in your narratives. Your fatal habit of looking at everything from the point of view of a story instead of as a scientific exercise has ruined what might have been an instructive and even classical series of demonstrations. You slur over work of the utmost finesse and delicacy, in order to dwell upon sensational details which may excite, but cannot possibly instruct, the reader."

"Why do you not write them yourself?" I said, with some bitterness.

"I will, my dear Watson, I will."

Holmes and Watson,
The Abbey Grange

"Come, come, sir," said Holmes, laughing. "You are like my friend, Dr. Watson, who has a bad habit of telling his stories wrong end foremost."

Holmes to Scott Eccles,
Wisteria Lodge

"I will do nothing serious without my trusted comrade and biographer at my elbow."

Holmes to Watson,
The Bruce-Partington Plans

And here it is that I miss my Watson. By cunning questions and ejaculations of wonder he could elevate my simple art, which is but systematized common sense, into a prodigy.

Holmes on Watson,
The Blanched Soldier

"Susan is a country girl ..."

"There is a wonderful sympathy and freemasonry among horsy men. Be one of them, and you will know all that there is to know."

Holmes to Watson,
A Scandal in Bohemia

Our visitor bore every mark of being an average common-place British tradesman, obese, pompous, and slow.

Watson on Jabez Wilson,
The Red-Headed League

"Sorry to see that you've had the British workman in the house. He's a token of evil."

Holmes to Watson,
The Crooked Man

9

"Susan is a country girl," said he, "and you know the incredible stupidity of that class."

Prof. Coram to Holmes,
The Golden Pince-Nez

A measured step was heard upon the stairs, and a moment later a stout, tall, gray-whiskered and solemnly respectable person was ushered into the room. His life history was written in his heavy features and pompous manner. From his spats to his gold-rimmed spectacles he was a Conservative, a churchman, a good citizen, orthodox and conventional to the last degree.

Watson on Scott Eccles,
Wisteria Lodge

"It is a great wandering house, standing in a considerable park. I should judge it was of all sorts of ages and styles, starting on a half-timbered Elizabethan foundation and ending in a Victorian portico. Inside it was all panelling and tapestry and half-effaced old pictures, a house of shadows and mystery. There was a butler, Old Ralph, who seemed about the same age as the house, and there was his wife, who might have been older.

James M. Dodd to Holmes,
The Blanched Soldier

**"... there is nothing so unnatural
as the commonplace."**

"It is a mistake to confound strangeness with mystery. The most commonplace crime is often the most mysterious, because it presents no new or special features from which deductions may be drawn. This murder would have been infinitely more difficult to unravel had the body of the victim been simply found lying in the roadway without any of those outré and sensational accompaniments which have rendered it remarkable. These strange details, far from making the case more difficult, have really had the effect of making it less so."

Holmes to Insp. Gregson and Insp. Lestrade,
A Study in Scarlet, Part 1, Chap. 7

"I have already explained to you that what is out of the common is usually a guide rather than a hindrance. In solving a problem of this sort, the grand thing is to be able to reason backward."

Holmes to Watson,
A Study in Scarlet, Part 2, Chap. 7

"I know, my dear Watson, that you share my love of all that is bizarre and outside the conventions and humdrum routine of everyday life. You have shown your relish for it by the enthusiasm which has prompted you to chronicle, and, if you will excuse my saying so, somewhat to embellish so many of my own little adventures."

Holmes to Watson,
The Red-Headed League

"As a rule," said Holmes, "the more bizarre a thing is the less mysterious it proves to be. It is your commonplace, featureless crimes which are really puzzling, just as a commonplace face is the most difficult to identify.

Holmes to Watson,
The Red-Headed League

"My life is spent in one long effort to escape from the commonplaces of existence. These little problems help me to do so."

Holmes to Watson,
The Red-Headed League

"Depend upon it, there is nothing so unnatural as the commonplace."

Holmes to Watson,
A Case of Identity

"It seems, from what I gather, to be one of those simple cases which are so extremely difficult."
"That sounds a little paradoxical."

11

"But it is profoundly true. Singularity is almost invariably a clue. The more featureless and commonplace a crime is, the more difficult it is to bring it home."

Holmes to Watson,
Boscombe Valley

"Was ever such a dreary, dismal, unprofitable world? See how the yellow fog swirls down the street and drifts across the dun-coloured houses. What could be more hopelessly prosaic and material?"

Holmes to Watson,
The Sign of Four, Chap. 1

"Crime is commonplace, existence is commonplace, and no qualities save those which are commonplace have any function upon earth."

Holmes to Watson,
The Sign of Four, Chap. 1

"Ah, me! It's a wicked world."

To all the world he was the man of violence, half animal and half demon; but to her he always remained the little willful boy of her own girlhood, the child who had clung to her hand. Evil indeed is the man who has not one woman to mourn him.

Watson on Selden, the convict,
The Hound of the Baskervilles, Chap. 13

"There are no crimes and no criminals in these days," he said, querulously.

Holmes to Watson,
A Study in Scarlet, Part 1, Chap. 2

"Like most clever criminals, he may be too confident in his own cleverness and imagine that he has completely deceived us."

Holmes to Watson, on Henry Stapleton,
The Hound of the Baskervilles, Chap. 13

"You have heard me remark that the strangest and most unique things are very often connected not with the larger but with the smaller crimes, and occasionally, indeed, where there is room for doubt whether any positive crime has been committed."

Holmes to Watson,
The Red-Headed League

"Smart fellow, that," observed Holmes as we walked away. "He is, in my judgment, the fourth smartest man in London, and for daring I am not sure that he has not a claim to be third."

Holmes on Vincent Spaulding,
The Red-Headed League

"The larger crimes are apt to be the simpler, for the bigger the crime the more obvious, as a rule, is the motive."

Holmes to Watson,
A Case of Identity

"No, no. No crime," said Sherlock Holmes, laughing. "Only one of those whimsical little incidents which will happen when you have four million human beings all jostling each other within the space of a few square miles. Amid the action and reaction of so dense a swarm of humanity, every possible combination of events may be expected to take place, and many a little problem will be presented which may be striking and bizarre without being criminal."

Holmes to Watson,
The Blue Carbuncle

"Well, Watson, I love to come to grips with my man. I like to meet him eye to eye and read for myself the stuff that he is made of."

Holmes to Watson,
The Illustrious Client

"I should be very much obliged if you would slip your revolver into your pocket. An Eley's No. 2 is an excellent argument

13

with gentlemen who can twist steel pokers into knots. That and a toothbrush are, I think all that we need."

Holmes to Watson,
The Speckled Band

"No violence, gentlemen – no violence, I beg of you! Consider the furniture!"

Holmes to Count Negretto Sylvius and Sam Merton,
The Mazarin Stone

"Ah, me! It's a wicked world, and when a clever man turns his brains to crime it is the worst of all."

Holmes to Watson and Helen Stoner,
The Speckled Band

"But, indeed, if you are trivial, I cannot blame you, for the days of the great cases are past. Man, or at least criminal man, has lost all enterprise and originality. As to my own little practice, it seems to be degenerating into an agency for recovering lost lead pencils and giving advice to young ladies from boarding-schools."

Holmes to Watson,
The Copper Beeches

"Do you know, Watson," said he, "that it is one of the curses of a mind with a turn like mine that I must look at everything with reference to my own special subject. You look at these scattered houses, and you are impressed by their beauty. I look at them, and the only thought which comes to me is a feeling of their isolation and of the impunity with which crime may be committed there."

Holmes and Watson,
The Copper Beeches

"I assure you that the most winning woman I ever knew was hanged for poisoning three little children for their insurance money, and the most repellent man of my acquaintance is a philanthropist who has spent nearly a quarter of a million upon the London poor."

Holmes to Watson,
The Sign of Four, Chap. 2

"The greatest schemer of all time, the organizer of every deviltry, the controlling brain of the underworld, a brain which might have made or marred the destiny of nations – that's the man!"

Holmes on Prof. Moriarty,
The Valley of Fear, Part 1, Chap. 1

"Everything comes in circles – even Professor Moriarty. Jonathan Wild was the hidden force of the London criminals, to whom he sold his brains and his organization on a fifteen per cent commission. The old wheel turns, and the same spoke comes up. It's all been done before, and will be again."

Holmes to Insp. MacDonald,
The Valley of Fear, Part 1, Chap. 2

"The most difficult crime to track is the one which is purposeless."

Holmes to Watson,
The Naval Treaty

"He is the Napoleon of crime, Watson. He is the organizer of half that is evil and of nearly all that is undetected in this great city. He is a genius, a philosopher, an abstract thinker. He has a brain of the first order. He sits motionless, like a spider in the centre of its web, but that web has a thousand radiations, and he knows well every quiver of each of them."

Holmes to Watson on Prof. Moriarty,
The Final Problem

"You crossed my path on the fourth of January," said he. "On the twenty-third you incommoded me; by the middle of February I was seriously inconvenienced by you; at the end of March I was absolutely hampered in my plans; and now, at the close of April, I find myself placed in such a position through your continual persecution that I am in positive danger of losing my liberty. The situation is becoming an impossible one."

Prof. Moriarty to Holmes,
The Final Problem

As the gleam of the street-lamps flashed upon his austere features, I saw that his brows were drawn down in thought and his thin lips compressed. I knew not what wild beast we were about to hunt down in the dark jungle of criminal London, but I was well assured, from the bearing of this master huntsman, that the adventure was a most grave one – while the sardonic smile which occasionally broke through his ascetic gloom boded little good for the object of our quest.

Watson on Holmes,
The Empty House

"You fiend!" he kept on muttering. "You clever, clever fiend!"

Col. Sebastian Moran to Holmes,
The Empty House

"The worst man in London. ... He is the king of all the blackmailers. Heaven help the man, and still more the woman, whose secret and reputation come into the power of Milverton!

With a smiling face and a heart of marble, he will squeeze and squeeze until he has drained them dry. The fellow is a genius in his way, and would have made his mark in some more savoury trade."

> Holmes on Charles Augustus Milverton,
> *Charles Augustus Milverton*

"I should not sit here smoking with you if I thought that you were a common criminal, you may be sure of that. Be frank with me and we may do some good. Play tricks with me, and I'll crush you."

> Holmes to Capt. Jack Crocker,
> *The Abbey Grange*

"The London criminal is certainly a dull fellow," said he in the querulous voice of the sportsman whose game has failed him. "Look out of this window, Watson. See how the figures loom up, are dimly seen, and then blend once more into the cloud-bank. The thief or the murderer could roam London on such a day as the tiger does the jungle, unseen until he pounces, and then evident only to his victim."

> Holmes to Watson,
> *The Bruce-Partington Plans*

"It is my business to follow the details of Continental crime."

> Holmes to Sir James Damery,
> *The Illustrious Client*

"A complex mind," said Holmes. "All great criminals have that. My old friend Charlie Peace was a violin virtuoso. Wainwright was no mean artist. I could quote many more."

> Holmes to Sir James Damery,
> *The Illustrious Client*

"Amberley excelled at chess – one mark, Watson, of the scheming mind."

> Holmes to Watson on Josiah Amberley,
> *The Retired Colourman*

17

"You speak of danger ..."

You may remember the old Persian saying, 'There is danger for him who taketh the tiger cub, and danger also for whoso snatches a delusion from a woman.' There is as much sense in Hafiz as in Horace, and as much knowledge of the world."

Holmes to Watson,
A Case of Identity

"There will probably be some small unpleasantness."

Holmes to Watson,
A Scandal in Bohemia

"It seems to me to be a most dark and sinister business."

Watson to Holmes,
The Speckled Band

"There is something devilish in this, Watson."

Holmes to Watson,
The Sign of Four, Chap. 5

"The situation is desperate, but not hopeless."

Holmes to Watson,
The Second Stain

"You speak of danger. You have evidently seen more in these rooms than was visible to me."

"No, but I fancy that I may have deduced a little more. I imagine that you saw all that I did."

Watson and Holmes,
The Speckled Band

"Danger! What danger do you foresee?"

Holmes shook his head gravely. "It would cease to be a danger if we could define it."

Violet Hunter and Holmes,
The Copper Beeches

18

"It is stupidity rather than courage to refuse to recognize danger when it is close upon you."

> Holmes to Watson,
> *The Naval Treaty*

It is, indeed, a fearful place. The torrent, swollen by the melting snow, plunges into a tremendous abyss, from which the spray rolls up like the smoke from a burning house. The shaft into which the river hurls itself is an immense chasm, lined by glistening coal-black rock, and narrowing into a creaming, boiling pit of incalculable depth, which brims over and shoots the stream onward over its jagged lip. The long sweep of green water roaring forever down, and the thick flickering curtain of spray hissing forever upward, turn a man giddy with their constant whirl and clamour. We stood near the edge peering down at the gleam of the breaking water far below us against the black rocks, and listening to the half-human shout which came booming up with the spray out of the abyss.

> Watson on the Reichenbach Falls,
> *The Final Problem*

My first feeling of fear had passed away, and I thrilled now with a keener zest than I had ever enjoyed when we were the defenders of the law instead of its defiers. The high object of our mission, the consciousness that it was unselfish and chivalrous, the villainous character of our opponent, all added to the sporting interest of the adventure.

Far from feeling guilty, I rejoiced and exulted in our dangers.

> Watson on burglary,
> *Charles Augustus Milverton*

"There's an east wind coming, Watson."

> Holmes to Watson,
> *His Last Bow*

"There's an east wind coming all the same, such a wind as never blew on England yet. It will be cold and bitter, Watson, and a good many of us may wither before its blast. But it's God's own wind nonetheless, and a cleaner, better, stronger land will lie in the sunshine when the storm has cleared."

Holmes to Watson,
His Last Bow

"I have not all my facts yet ..."

"It is a capital mistake to theorize before you have all the evidence. It biases the judgment."

Holmes to Watson,
A Study in Scarlet, Part 1, Chap. 3

"There is nothing like first-hand evidence."

Holmes to Watson,
A Study in Scarlet, Part 1, Chap. 4

"I have no data yet. It is a capital mistake to theorize before one has data. Insensibly one begins to twist facts to suit theories, instead of theories to suit facts."

Holmes to Watson,
A Scandal in Bohemia

"I had," said he, "come to an entirely erroneous conclusion which shows, my dear Watson, how dangerous it always is to reason from insufficient data."

Holmes to Watson,
The Speckled Band

As to Holmes, I observed that he sat frequently for half an hour on end, with knitted brows and an abstracted air, but he swept the matter away with a wave of his hand when I mentioned it.

"Data! data! data!" he cried impatiently. "I can't make bricks without clay."

Watson on Holmes,
The Copper Beeches

"The temptation to form premature theories upon insufficient data is the bane of our profession."

Holmes to Insp. MacDonald,
The Valley of Fear, Part 1, Chap. 2

"I have not all my facts yet, but I do not think there are any insuperable difficulties. Still, it is an error to argue in front of your data. You find yourself insensibly twisting them round to fit your theories."

Holmes to Watson,
Wisteria Lodge

"There is nothing more deceptive than an obvious fact."

Holmes to Watson,
Boscombe Valley

"I find it hard enough to tackle facts, Holmes, without flying away after theories and fancies."

Insp. Lestrade to Holmes,
Boscombe Valley

"Some facts should be suppressed, or, at least, a just sense of proportion should be observed in treating them."

Holmes to Watson,
The Sign of Four, Chap. 1

"It is of the highest importance in the art of detection to be able to recognize, out of a number of facts, which are incidental and which vital. Otherwise your energy and attention must be dissipated instead of being concentrated."

Holmes to Col Hayter,
The Reigate Puzzle

The Science of Deduction

"I ought to know by this time that when a fact appears to be opposed to a long train of deductions, it invariably proves to be capable of bearing some other interpretation.

Holmes to Watson,
A Study in Scarlet, Part 1, Chap. 7

"When I hear you give your reasons," I remarked, "the thing always appears to me to be so ridiculously simple that I could easily do it myself, though at each successive instance of your reasoning I am baffled until you explain your process."

Watson to Holmes, .
A Scandal in Bohemia

There was something in his masterly grasp of a situation, and his keen, incisive reasoning, which made it a pleasure to me to study his system of work, and to follow the quick, subtle methods by which he disentangled the most inextricable mysteries.

Watson on Holmes,
A Scandal in Bohemia

"I can see nothing," said I, handing it back to my friend.

"On the contrary, Watson, you can see everything. You fail, however, to reason from what you see. You are too timid in drawing your inferences."

Watson and Holmes,
The Blue Carbuncle

"How did you deduce that this man was intellectual?"

For answer, Holmes clapped the hat upon his head. It came right over the forehead and settled upon the bridge of his nose.

"It is a question of cubic capacity," said he; "a man with so large a brain must have something in it."

Watson and Holmes,
The Blue Carbuncle

"You see, Watson, our little deductions have suddenly assumed a much more important and less innocent aspect."

Holmes to Watson,
The Blue Carbuncle

"They have been identified as her clothes, and it seemed to me that if the clothes were there the body would not be far off."

"By the same brilliant reasoning, every man's body is to be found in the neighbourhood of his wardrobe."

Insp. Lestrade and Holmes,
The Noble Bachelor

"What do the public, the great unobservant public, who could hardly tell a weaver by his tooth or a compositor by his left thumb, care about the finer shades of analysis and deduction!"

Holmes to Watson,
The Copper Beeches

"Perhaps I should have said 'replaced it there,' " said Holmes.

"You will remember, Inspector MacDonald, that I was somewhat struck by the absence of a dumb-bell. I drew your attention to it; but with the pressure of other events you had hardly the time to give it the consideration which would have enabled you to draw deductions from it. When water is near and a weight is missing it is not a very far-fetched supposition that something has been sunk in the water."

Holmes to Insp. MacDonald,
The Valley of Fear, Part 1, Chap. 6

"You may not be aware that the deduction of a man's age from his writing is one which has been brought to considerable accuracy by experts. In normal cases one can place a man in his true decade with tolerable confidence."

Holmes to Col. Hayter,
The Reigate Puzzle

"We must look for consistency. Where there is a want of it we must suspect deception."

Holmes to Watson,
Thor Bridge

"To a great mind, nothing is little."

"Ha!" cried Gregson, in a relieved voice; "you should never neglect a chance, however small it may seem."
"To a great mind, nothing is little," remarked Holmes, sententiously.

Insp. Gregson and Holmes,
A Study in Scarlet, Part 1, Chap. 6

"By a man's fingernails, by his coat-sleeve, by his boots, by his trouser-knees, by the callosities of his forefinger and thumb, by his expression, by his shirt-cuffs – by each of these things a man's calling is plainly revealed.

Holmes to Watson,
A Study in Scarlet, Part 1, Chap. 2

"They say that genius is an infinite capacity for taking pains," he remarked with a smile. "It's a very bad definition, but it does apply to detective work."

Holmes to Insp. Gregson and Insp. Lestrade,
A Study in Scarlet, Part 1, Chap. 3

"Why, the height of a man, in nine cases out of ten, can be told from the length of his stride. It is a simple calculation enough, though there is no use my boring you with figures."

Holmes to Watson,
A Study in Scarlet, Part 1, Chap. 4

"It is a curious thing," remarked Holmes, "that a typewriter has really quite as much individuality as a man's handwriting. Unless they are quite new, no two of them write exactly alike. Some letters get more worn than others, and some wear only on one side."

Holmes to James Windibank,
A Case of Identity

"Dear me, Watson, is it possible that you have not penetrated the fact that the case hangs upon the missing dumb-bell?"

Holmes to Watson,
The Valley of Fear, Part 1, Chap. 6

"It is one of those cases where the art of the reasoner should be used rather for the sifting of details than for the acquiring of fresh evidence."

Holmes to Watson,
Silver Blaze

"I pay a good deal of attention to matters of detail, as you may have observed."

Holmes to Lestrade,
The Norwood Builder

"It seems to me to have only one drawback, Hopkins, and that is that it is intrinsically impossible. Have you tried to drive a harpoon through a body? No? Tut, tut, my dear sir, you must really pay attention to these details."

Holmes to Insp. Stanley Hopkins,
Black Peter

"It would be difficult to name any articles which afford a finer field for inference than a pair of glasses."

Holmes to Insp. Stanley Hopkins,
The Golden Pince-Nez

"As a medical man, you are aware, Watson, that there is no part of the body which varies so much as the human ear. Each ear is as a rule quite distinctive and differs from all other ones."

Holmes to Watson,
The Cardboard Box

"Why do you not solve it yourself, Mycroft? You can see as far as I."

"Possibly, Sherlock. But it is a question of getting details. Give me your details, and from an armchair I will return you an excellent expert opinion. But to run here and run there, to cross-question railway guards, and lie on my face with a lens to my eye – it is not my *métier*. No, you are the one man who can clear the matter up."

Holmes and Mycroft Holmes,
The Bruce-Partington Plans

"Always look at the hands first, Watson. Then cuffs, trouser-knees, and boots."

Holmes to Watson,
The Creeping Man

"There is no branch of detective science which is so important and so much neglected as the art of tracing footsteps."

Holmes to Watson,
A Study in Scarlet, Part 2, Chap. 7

"The detection of types is one of the most elementary branches of knowledge to the special expert in crime, though I confess that once when I was very young I confused the *Leeds Mercury* with the *Western Morning News*."

Holmes to James Mortimer and Sir Henry Baskerville,
The Hound of the Baskervilles, Chap. 4

In [the Camberwell poisoning case], as may be remembered, Sherlock Holmes was able, by winding up the dead man's watch, to prove that it had been wound up two hours before, and that therefore the deceased had gone to bed within that time – a deduction which was of the greatest importance in clearing up the case.

Watson on Holmes,
The Five Orange Pips

"Not invisible but unnoticed, Watson. You did not know where to look, and so you missed all that was important. I can never bring you to realize the importance of sleeves, the suggestiveness of thumbnails, or the great issues that may hang from a bootlace."

Holmes to Watson,
A Case of Identity

"Well, I have a trade of my own ..."

"No man lives or has ever lived who has brought the same amount of study and of natural talent to the detection of crime which I have done. And what is the result? There is no crime to detect, or, at most, some bungling villainy with a motive so transparent that even a Scotland Yard official can see through it."

Holmes to Watson,
A Study in Scarlet, Part 1, Chap. 2

"Well, I have a trade of my own. I suppose I am the only one in the world. I'm a consulting detective."

Holmes to Watson,
A Study in Scarlet, Part 1, Chap. 2

"Now, in my opinion, Dupin was a very inferior fellow."

Holmes to Watson, on Poe's detective,
A Study in Scarlet, Part 1, Chap. 2

"Lecoq was a miserable bungler," he said, in an angry voice; "he had only one thing to recommend him, and that was his energy."

Holmes to Watson, on Gaboriau's detective,
A Study in Scarlet, Part 1, Chap. 2

"You have brought detection as near an exact science as it ever will be brought in this world."

Watson to Holmes,
A Study in Scarlet, Part 1, Chap. 4

"It's the Baker Street division of the detective police force," said my companion gravely; and as he spoke there rushed into the room half a dozen of the dirtiest and most ragged street Arabs that ever I clapped eyes on.

Holmes to Watson,
A Study in Scarlet, Part 1, Chap. 6

"There's more work to be got out of one of those little beggars than out of a dozen of the force," Holmes remarked. "The mere sight of an official-looking person seals men's lips. These youngsters, however, go everywhere and hear everything. They are as sharp as needles, too; all they want is organization."

Holmes to Watson,
A Study in Scarlet, Part 1, Chap. 6

"I believe in hard work and not in sitting by the fire spinning fine theories."

Insp. Lestrade to Holmes,
The Noble Bachelor

"Detection is, or ought to be, an exact science and should be treated in the same cold and unemotional manner. You have attempted to tinge it with romanticism, which produces much the same effect as if you worked a love-story or an elopement into the fifth proposition of Euclid."

Holmes to Watson,
The Sign of Four, Chap. 1

"He possesses two out of the three qualities necessary for the ideal detective. He has the power of observation and that of deduction. He is only wanting in knowledge, and that may come in time."

Holmes to Watson on François le Villard,
The Sign of Four, Chap. 1

"All knowledge comes useful to the detective."

Holmes to Watson,
The Valley of Fear, Part 1, Chap. 2

"Breadth of view, my dear Mr. Mac, is one of the essentials of our profession. The interplay of ideas and the oblique uses of knowledge are often of extraordinary interest."

Holmes to Insp. MacDonald,
The Valley of Fear, Part 1, Chap. 6

"Pipes are occasionally of extraordinary interest," said he. "Nothing has more individuality, save perhaps watches and boot-laces."

Holmes to Watson,
The Yellow Face

29

"I don't know how you manage this, Mr. Holmes, but it seems to me that all the detectives of fact and of fancy would be children in your hands."

> Justice Trevor to Holmes,
> *The "Gloria Scott"*

"It is always awkward doing business with an alias."

He had at least five small refuges in different parts of London, in which he was able to change his personality.

> Watson on Holmes,
> *Black Peter*

"My eyes have been trained to examine faces and not their trimmings. It is the first quality of a criminal investigator that he should see through a disguise."

> Holmes to Watson,
> *The Hound of the Baskervilles*, Chap. 13

He disappeared into his bedroom and returned in a few minutes in the character of an amiable and simple-minded Nonconformist clergyman.

> Watson on Holmes,
> *A Scandal in Bohemia*

"No, no; the real name," said Holmes sweetly. "It is always awkward doing business with an alias."

> Holmes to James Ryder,
> *The Blue Carbuncle*

"When a doctor goes wrong ..."

The public not unnaturally goes on the principle that he who would heal others must himself be whole, and looks askance at the curative powers of the man whose own case is beyond the reach of his drugs.

> Watson,
> *The Stock-Broker's Clerk*

"When a doctor does go wrong he is the first of criminals. He has nerve and he has knowledge."

> Holmes to Watson,
> *The Speckled Band*

"... the curious incident of the dog in the night-time."

"Yes, a queer mongrel with a most amazing power of scent. I would rather have Toby's help than that of the whole detective force of London."

> Holmes to Watson on Toby, the dog,
> *The Sign of Four*, Chap. 6

"Mr. Holmes, they were the footprints of a gigantic hound!"

> Charles Mortimer to Holmes,
> *The Hound of the Baskervilles*, Chap. 2

A hound it was, an enormous coal-black hound, but not such a hound as mortal eyes have ever seen. Fire burst from its open mouth, its eyes glowed with a smouldering glare, its muzzle and hackles and dewlap were outlined in flickering flame. Never in the delirious dream of a disordered brain could anything more savage, more appalling, more hellish be conceived than that dark form and savage face which broke upon us out of the wall of fog.

> Watson,
> *The Hound of the Baskervilles*, Chap. 14

"Is there any point to which you would wish to draw my attention?"

"To the curious incident of the dog in the night-time."

"The dog did nothing in the night-time."

"That was the curious incident," remarked Sherlock Holmes.

Insp. Gregory and Holmes,
Silver Blaze

"A dog reflects the family life. Whoever saw a frisky dog in a gloomy family, or a sad dog in a happy one? Snarling people have snarling dogs, dangerous people have dangerous ones. And their passing moods may reflect the passing moods of others.

Holmes to Watson,
The Creeping Man

"What have you done, Holmes?" I asked.

"A threadbare and venerable device, but useful upon occasion. I walked into the doctor's yard this morning, and shot my syringe full of aniseed over the hind wheel. A draghound will follow aniseed from here to John o' Groat's, and our friend, Armstrong, would have to drive through the Cam before he would shake Pompey off his trail."

Watson and Holmes,
The Missing Three-Quarter

"... a seven-per-cent solution."

Isa Whitney, brother of the late Elias Whitney, D.D., Principal of the Theological College of St. George's, was much addicted to opium. The habit grew upon him, as I understand, from some foolish freak when he was at college; for having read De Quincey's description of his dreams and sensations, he had drenched his tobacco with laudanum in an attempt to produce the same effects. He found, as so many more have done, that the practice is easier to attain than to get rid of, and for many years he continued to be a slave to the drug, an object of mingled horror and pity to his friends and relatives. I can see him now, with yellow, pasty face, drooping lids, and pin-point pupils, all huddled in a chair, the wreck and ruin of a noble man.

Watson on Isa Whitney,
The Man with the Twisted Lip

"I suppose, Watson," said he, "that you imagine that I have added opium-smoking to cocaine injections, and all the other little weaknesses on which you have favoured me with your medical views."

Holmes to Watson,
The Man with the Twisted Lip

"Which is it to-day," I asked, "morphine or cocaine?"

He raised his eyes languidly from the old black-letter volume which he had opened.

"It is cocaine," he said, "a seven-per-cent solution. Would you care to try it?"

Watson and Holmes,
The Sign of Four, Chap. 1

"Perhaps you are right, Watson," he said. "I suppose that its influence is physically a bad one. I find it, however, so transcendently stimulating and clarifying to the mind that its secondary action is a matter of small moment."

Holmes to Watson,
The Sign of Four, Chap. 1

Save for the occasional use of cocaine, he had no vices, and he only turned to the drug as a protest against the monotony of existence when cases were scanty and the papers uninteresting.

Watson on Holmes,
The Yellow Face

"Interesting, though elementary."

"All this is amusing, though rather elementary."

Holmes to Watson,
A Case of Identity

"Interesting, though elementary,"

Holmes to Watson,
The Hound of the Baskervilles, Chap. 1

"Elementary," said he. "It is one of those instances where the reasoner can produce an effect which seems remarkable to his neighbour, because the latter has missed the one little point which is the basis of the deduction."

Holmes to Watson,
The Crooked Man

"The train of reasoning is not very obscure, Watson," said Holmes with a mischievous twinkle. "It belongs to the same elementary class of deduction which I should illustrate if I were to ask you who shared your cab in your drive this morning."

Holmes to Watson,
Lady Francis Carfax

... a man who seldom took exercise ...

Sherlock Holmes was a man who seldom took exercise for exercise's sake. Few men were capable of greater muscular effort, and he was undoubtedly one of the finest boxers of his weight that I have ever seen; but he looked upon aimless bodily exertion as a waste of energy, and he seldom bestirred himself save where there was some professional object to be served. Then he was absolutely untiring and indefatigable.

Watson on Holmes,
The Yellow Face

"There can be no question, my dear Watson, of the value of exercise before breakfast."

Holmes to Watson,
Black Peter

The state of his health was not a matter in which he himself took the faintest interest, for his mental detachment was absolute.

Watson on Holmes,
The Devil's Foot

"Meanwhile we can thank our lucky fate which has rescued us for a few short hours from the insufferable fatigues of idleness."

Holmes to Watson,
Wisteria Lodge

"There are some trees ..."

"My dear Watson, you as a medical man are continually gaining light as to the tendencies of a child by the study of the parents. Don't you see that the converse is equally valid. I have frequently gained my first real insight into the character of parents by studying their children."

Holmes to Watson,
The Copper Beeches

"There are some trees, Watson, which grow to a certain height, and then suddenly develop some unsightly eccentricity. You will see it often in humans. I have a theory that the individual represents in his development the whole procession of his ancestors, and that such a sudden turn to good or evil stands for some strong influence which came into the line of his pedigree. The person becomes, as it were, the epitome of the history of his own family."

Holmes to Watson,
The Empty House

"A study of family portraits is enough to convert a man to the doctrine of reincarnation."

Holmes to Watson,
The Hound of the Baskervilles, Chap. 13

"Stand with me here upon the terrace ..."

"You amaze me, Holmes."

Watson to Holmes,
A Study in Scarlet, Part 1, Chap. 4

His manner was not effusive. It seldom was; but he was glad, I think, to see me.

> Watson on Holmes,
> *A Scandal in Bohemia*

"I have been too busy to think of food, and I am likely to be busier still this evening. By the way, Doctor, I shall want your co-operation."

"I shall be delighted."

"You don't mind breaking the law?"

"Not in the least."

"Nor running a chance of arrest?"

"Not in a good cause."

"Oh, the cause is excellent!"

"Then I am your man."

"I was sure that I might rely on you."

> Holmes and Watson,
> *A Scandal in Bohemia*

"It makes a considerable difference to me, having someone with me on whom I can thoroughly rely. Local aid is always either worthless or else biased.

> Holmes to Watson,
> *Boscombe Valley*

It was difficult to refuse any of Sherlock Holmes's requests, for they were always so exceedingly definite, and put forward with such a quiet air of mastery.

> Watson on Holmes,
> *The Man with the Twisted Lip*

The best and the wisest man whom I have ever known.

> Watson on Holmes,
> *The Final Problem*

"Stand with me here upon the terrace, for it may be the last quiet talk that we shall ever have."

> Holmes to Watson,
> *His Last Bow*

My friend has so often astonished me in the course of our adventures that it was with a sense of exultation that I realized how completely I had astonished him.

Watson on Holmes,
The Second Stain

I have so deep a respect for the extraordinary qualities of Holmes that I have always deferred to his wishes, even when I least understood them.

Watson on Holmes,
The Dying Detective

There was a curious secretive streak in the man which led to many dramatic effects, but left even his closest friends guessing as to what his exact plans might be. He pushed to an extreme the axiom that the only safe plotter was he who plotted alone. I was nearer to him than anyone else, and yet I was always conscious of the gap between.

Watson on Holmes,
The Illustrious Client

"You're not hurt, Watson? For God's sake, say that you are not hurt!"

It was worth a wound – it was worth many wounds – to know the depth of loyalty and love which lay behind that cold mask. The clear, hard eyes were dimmed for a moment, and the firm lips were shaking. For the one and only time I caught a glimpse of a great heart as well as of a great brain. All my years of humble but single-minded service culminated in that moment of revelation.

Holmes and Watson,
The Three Garridebs

The relations between us in those latter days were peculiar. He was a man of habits, narrow and concentrated habits, and I had become one of them. As an institution, I was like the violin, the shag tobacco, the old black pipe, the index books, and others perhaps less excusable.

Watson on Holmes,
The Creeping Man

"The game is afoot!"

"The plot thickens."

Holmes to Watson,
A Study in Scarlet, Part 1, Chap. 5

"Come, Watson, come!" he cried. "The game is afoot. Not a word! Into your clothes and come!"

Holmes to Watson,
The Abbey Grange

"Come at once if convenient – if inconvenient come all the same."

Holmes to Watson in a telegram,
The Creeping Man

Talent instantly recognizes genius.

Mediocrity knows nothing higher than itself; but talent instantly recognizes genius,

> Watson on Insp. Alec MacDonald and Holmes,
> *The Valley of Fear*, Part 1, Chap. 1

"What is the meaning of it, Watson?"

"I have hitherto confined my investigations to this world," said he. "In a modest way I have combated evil, but to take on the Father of Evil himself would, perhaps, be too ambitious a task."

> Holmes to James Mortimer,
> *The Hound of the Baskervilles*, Chap. 3

If my future were black, it was better surely to face it like a man than to attempt to brighten it by mere will-o'-the-wisps of the imagination.

> Watson,
> *The Sign of Four*, Chap. 2

"There is nothing in which deduction is so necessary as in religion," said he, leaning with his back against the shutters. "It can be built up as an exact science by the reasoner. Our highest assurance of the goodness of Providence seems to me to rest in the flowers. All other things, our powers, our desires, our food, are all really necessary for our existence in the first instance. But this rose is an extra. Its smell and its colour are an embellishment of life, not a condition of it. It is only goodness which gives extras, and so I say again that we have much to hope from the flowers."

> Holmes to Watson and Percy Phelps,
> *The Naval Treaty*

"What is the meaning of it, Watson?" said Holmes solemnly as he laid down the paper. "What object is served by this circle of misery and violence and fear? It must tend to some end, or else our universe is ruled by chance, which is unthinkable. But what end? There is the great standing perennial problem to which human reason is as far from an answer as ever."

Holmes to Watson,
The Cardboard Box

"You won't die in your bed, Holmes"
"I have often had the same idea. Does it matter very much?"

Count Negretto Sylvius and Holmes,
The Mazarin Stone

"When one tries to rise above Nature one is liable to fall below it. The highest type of man may revert to the animal if he leaves the straight road of destiny."

Holmes to Watson,
The Creeping Man

"The wages of sin, Watson – the wages of sin!" said he. "Sooner or later it will always come. God knows, there was sin enough."

Holmes to Watson,
The Illustrious Client

"The ways of fate are indeed hard to understand. If there is no some compensation hereafter, then the world is a cruel jest."

Holmes to Mrs. Ronder,
The Veiled Lodger

"Exactly, Watson. Pathetic and futile. But is not all life pathetic and futile? Is not his story a microcosm of the whole? We reach. We grasp. And what is left in our hands at the end? A shadow. Or worse than a shadow – misery."

Holmes to Watson,
The Retired Colourman

The stage lost a fine actor ...

It was not merely that Holmes changed his costume. His expression, his manner, his very soul seemed to vary with every fresh part that he assumed. The stage lost a fine actor, even as science lost an acute reasoner, when he became a specialist in crime.

Watson on Holmes,
A Scandal in Bohemia

"A certain selection and discretion must be used in producing a realistic effect."

Holmes to Watson,
A Case of Identity

"Watson insists that I am the dramatist in real life," said he. "Some touch of the artist wells up within me, and calls insistently for a well-staged performance. Surely our profession, Mr. Mac, would be a drab and sordid one if we did not sometimes set the scene so as to glorify our results. The blunt accusation, the brutal tap upon the shoulder – what can one make of such a denouement? But the quick inference, the subtle trap, the clever forecast of coming events, the triumphant vindication of bold theories – are these not the pride and the justification of our life's work?"

Holmes to Insp. MacDonald,
The Valley of Fear, Part 1, Chap. 6

"Watson here will tell you that I never can resist a touch of the dramatic."

Holmes to Percy Phelps,
The Naval Treaty

"The best way of successfully acting a part is to be it."

Holmes to Culverton Smith,
The Dying Detective

"Old Baron Dowson said the night before he was hanged that in my case what the law had gained the stage had lost."

Holmes to Count Negretto Sylvius
The Mazarin Stone

"You'll find him a knotty problem ..."

"He is not a man that it is easy to draw out, though he can be communicative enough when the fancy seizes him."
> Stamford to Watson on Holmes,
> *A Study in Scarlet*, Part 1, Chap. 1

"It is not easy to express the inexpressible,"
> Stamford to Watson on Holmes,
> *A Study in Scarlet*, Part 1, Chap. 1

"Holmes is a little too scientific for my tastes – it approaches to cold-bloodedness. I could imagine his giving a friend a little pinch of the latest vegetable alkaloid, not out of malevolence, you understand, but simply out of a spirit of inquiry in order to have an accurate idea of the effects.
> Stamford to Watson on Holmes,
> *A Study in Scarlet*, Part 1, Chap. 1

"He appears to have a passion for definite and exact knowledge."
> Stamford to Watson on Holmes,
> *A Study in Scarlet*, Part 1, Chap. 1

"You must study him, then," Stamford said, as he bade me goodbye. "You'll find him a knotty problem, though."
> Stamford to Watson on Holmes,
> *A Study in Scarlet*, Part 1, Chap. 1

One of Sherlock Holmes's defects – if, indeed, one may call it a defect – was that he was exceedingly loath to communicate his full plans to any other person until the instant of their fulfillment. Partly it came no doubt from his own masterful nature, which loved to dominate and surprise those who were around him. Partly also from his professional caution, which urged him never to take any chances.
> Watson on Holmes,
> *The Hound of the Baskervilles*, Chap. 14

"I know you, you scoundrel! I have heard of you before. You are Holmes, the meddler."

My friend smiled.

"Holmes, the busybody!"

His smile broadened.

"Holmes, the Scotland Yard Jack-in-office!"

Holmes chuckled heartily. "Your conversation is most entertaining," said he. "When you go out close the door, for there is a decided draught."

Dr. Grimseby Roylott and Holmes,
The Speckled Band

More than once during the years that I had lived with him in Baker Street I had observed that a small vanity underlay my companion's quiet and didactic manner.

Watson on Holmes,
The Sign of Four, Chap. 1

"You really are an automaton – a calculating machine," I cried. "There is something positively inhuman in you at times."

Watson to Holmes,
The Sign of Four, Chap. 2

"I have a curious constitution. I never remember feeling tired by work, though idleness exhausts me completely."

Holmes to Watson,
The Sign of Four, Chap. 8

"There are in me the makings of a very fine loafer, and also of a pretty spry sort of a fellow."

Holmes to Watson,
The Sign of Four, Chap. 12

"Really, Holmes," said I severely, "you are a little trying at times."

Watson to Holmes,
The Valley of Fear, Part 1, Chap. 1

Without having a tinge of cruelty in his singular composition, he was undoubtedly callous from long overstimulation. Yet, if his emotions were dulled, his intellectual perceptions were exceedingly active.

Watson on Holmes,
The Valley of Fear, Part 1, Chap. 2

My friend, who loved above all things precision and concentration of thought, resented anything which distracted his attention from the matter in hand.

Watson on Holmes,
The Solitary Cyclist

It was one of my friend's most obvious weaknesses that he was impatient with less alert intelligences than his own.

Watson on Holmes,
The Bruce-Partington Plans

"My old friend here will tell you that I have an impish habit of practical joking."

Holmes to Lord Cantlemere,
The Mazarin Stone

For an instant the veil had lifted upon his keen, intense nature, but for an instant only. When I glanced again his face had resumed that red-Indian composure which had made so many regard him as a machine rather than a man.

Watson on Holmes,
The Crooked Man

"Thank you," said he, as he replaced the glass. "It is the second most interesting object that I have seen in the North."
"And the first?"
Holmes folded up his cheque and placed it carefully in his notebook. "I am a poor man," said he, as he patted it affectionately, and thrust it into the depths of his inner pocket.

Holmes and the Duke of Holdernesse,
The Priory School

"I would have made a highly efficient criminal"

"Well, well, my dear fellow, be it so. We have shared this same room for some years, and it would be amusing if we ended by sharing the same cell. You know, Watson, I don't mind confessing to you that I have always had an idea that I would have made a highly efficient criminal. This is the chance of my lifetime in that direction."

Holmes to Watson,
Charles Augustus Milverton

45

"It is fortunate for this community that I am not a criminal."

Holmes to Watson,
The Bruce-Partington Plans

"Burglary has always been an alternative profession had I cared to adopt it, and I have little doubt that I should have come to the front."

Holmes to Insp. MacKinnon,
The Retired Colourman

"... his habits were regular."

His very person and appearance were such as to strike the attention of the most casual observer.

Watson on Holmes,
A Study in Scarlet, Part 1, Chap. 2

Holmes was certainly not a difficult man to live with. He was quiet in his ways, and his habits were regular.

Watson on Holmes,
A Study in Scarlet, Part 1, Chap. 2

Holmes chuckled and wriggled in his chair, as was his habit when in high spirits.

Watson on Holmes,
The Red-Headed League

Sherlock Holmes was, as I expected, lounging about his sitting-room in his dressing-gown, reading the agony column of *The Times* and smoking his before-breakfast pipe, which was composed of all the plugs and dottles left from his smokes of the day before, all carefully dried and collected on the corner of the mantelpiece.

Watson on Holmes,
The Engineer's Thumb

An anomaly which often struck me in the character of my friend Sherlock Holmes was that, although in his methods of thought he was the neatest and most methodical of mankind, and although also he affected a certain quiet primness of dress, he was nonetheless in his personal habits one of the most untidy men that ever drove a fellow lodger to distraction. Not that I am in the least conventional in that respect myself. The rough-and-tumble work in Afghanistan, coming on the top of natural Bohemianism of disposition, has made me rather more lax than befits a medical man. But with me there is a limit, and when I find a man who keeps his cigars in the coal-scuttle, his tobacco in the toe end of a Persian slipper, and his unanswered correspondence transfixed by a jack-knife into the very centre of his wooden mantelpiece, then I begin to give myself virtuous airs.

Watson on Holmes,
The Musgrave Ritual

Our chambers were always full of chemicals and of criminal relics which had a way of wandering into unlikely positions, and of turning up in the butter-dish or in even less desirable places.

Watson,
The Musgrave Ritual

He had a horror of destroying documents, especially those which were connected with his past cases, and yet it was only once in every year or two that he would muster energy to docket and arrange them.

Watson on Holmes,
The Musgrave Ritual

My friend had no breakfast himself, for it was one of his peculiarities that in his more intense moments he would permit himself no food, and I have known him presume upon his iron strength until he has fainted from pure inanition. "At present I cannot spare energy and nerve force for digestion," he would say in answer to my medical remonstrances.

Watson on Holmes,
The Norwood Builder

47

Mrs. Hudson, the landlady of Sherlock Holmes, was a long-suffering woman. Not only was her first-floor flat invaded at all hours by throngs of singular and often undesirable characters but her remarkable lodger showed an eccentricity and irregularity in his life which must have sorely tried her patience. His incredible untidiness, his addiction to music at strange hours, his occasional revolver practice within doors, his weird and often malodorous scientific experiments, and the atmosphere of violence and danger which hung around him made him the very worst tenant in London. On the other hand, his payments were princely. I have no doubt that the house might have been purchased at the price which Holmes paid for his rooms during the years that I was with him.

Watson on Holmes,
The Dying Detective

"It is my business to know things."

"His studies are very desultory and eccentric, but he has amassed a lot of out-of-the-way knowledge which would astonish his professors."

Stamford on Holmes,
A Study in Scarlet, Part 1, Chap. 1

His ignorance was as remarkable as his knowledge. Of contemporary literature, philosophy and politics he appeared to know next to nothing. ... My surprise reached a climax, however, when I found incidentally that he was ignorant of the Copernican Theory and of the composition of the Solar System. That any civilized human being in this nineteenth century should not be aware that the earth travelled round the sun appeared to me to be such an extraordinary fact that I could hardly realize it.

Watson on Holmes,
A Study in Scarlet, Part 1, Chap. 2

"What the deuce is it to me?" he interrupted impatiently: "you say that we go round the sun. If we went round the moon it would not make a pennyworth of difference to me or to my work."

Holmes to Watson, on Copernican Theory,
A Study in Scarlet, Part 1, Chap. 2

It struck me as being a remarkable mixture of shrewdness and of absurdity.

Watson on Holmes,
A Study in Scarlet, Part 1, Chap. 2

"It was easier to know it than to explain why I know it. If you were asked to prove that two and two made four, you might find some difficulty, and yet you are quite sure of the fact."

Holmes to Watson,
A Study in Scarlet, Part 1, Chap. 3

"I have now in my hands," my companion said, confidently, "all the threads which have formed such a tangle."

Holmes to Insp. Gregson and Insp. Lestrade,
A Study in Scarlet, Part 1, Chap. 7

"My name is Sherlock Holmes. It is my business to know what other people don't know."

Holmes to James Ryder,
The Blue Carbuncle

Holmes could talk exceedingly well when he chose, and that night he did choose. He appeared to be in a state of nervous exaltation. I have never known him so brilliant. He spoke on a quick succession of subjects – on miracle plays, on medieval pottery, on Stradivarius violins, on the Buddhism of Ceylon, and on the warships of the future – handling each as though he had made a special study of it.

Watson on Holmes,
The Sign of Four, Chap. 10

"I have taken to living by my wits."

Holmes to Reginald Musgrave,
The Musgrave Ritual

"I have some knowledge, however, of baritsu, or the Japanese system of wrestling, which has more than once been very useful to me."

Holmes to Watson,
The Empty House

"It is my business to know things. That is my trade."

Holmes to Col. Emsworth,
The Blanched Soldier

You will know, or Watson has written in vain, that I hold a vast store of out-of-the-way knowledge without scientific system, but very available for the needs of my work. My mind is like a crowded box-room with packets of all sorts stowed away therein – so many that I may well have but a vague perception of what was there.

Holmes,
The Lion's Mane

"I get in the dumps at times ..."

Sherlock Holmes had, in a very remarkable degree, the power of detaching his mind at will. For two hours the strange business in which we had been involved appeared to be forgotten, and he was entirely absorbed in the pictures of the modern Belgian masters. He would talk of nothing but art, of which he had the crudest ideas, from our leaving the gallery until we found ourselves at the Northumberland Hotel.

Watson on Holmes,
The Hound of the Baskervilles, Chap. 5

He continued to walk up and down the room with his head sunk on his chest and his brows drawn down, as was his habit when lost in thought.

Watson on Holmes,
A Study in Scarlet, Part 1, Chap. 7

"I get in the dumps at times, and don't open my mouth for days on end. You must not think I am sulky when I do that. Just let me alone, and I'll soon be right."

Holmes to Watson,
A Study in Scarlet, Part 1, Chap. 1

Nothing could exceed his energy when the working fit was upon him; but now and again a reaction would seize him, and for days on end he would lie upon the sofa in the sitting-room, hardly uttering a word or moving a muscle from morning to night. On these occasions I have noticed such a dreamy, vacant expression in his eyes, that I might have suspected him of being addicted to the use of some narcotic, had not the temperance and cleanliness of his whole life forbidden such a notion.

Watson on Holmes,
A Study in Scarlet, Part 1, Chap. 2

51

Surely no man would work so hard or attain such precise information unless he had some definite end in view.

Watson on Holmes,
A Study in Scarlet, Part 1, Chap. 2

His eyes had assumed the vacant, lacklustre expression which showed mental abstraction.

Watson on Holmes,
A Study in Scarlet, Part 1, Chap. 3

"I am the most incurably lazy devil that ever stood in shoe leather – that is, when the fit is on me, for I can be spry enough at times."

Holmes to Watson,
A Study in Scarlet, Part 1, Chap. 3

Holmes had taken out his watch, and as minute followed minute without result, an expression of the utmost chagrin and disappointment appeared upon his features. He gnawed his lip, drummed his fingers upon the table, and showed every other symptom of acute impatience.

Watson on Holmes,
A Study in Scarlet, Part 1, Chap. 7

"What you do in this world is a matter of no consequence," returned my companion, bitterly. "The question is, what can you make people believe that you have done?"

Holmes to Watson,
A Study in Scarlet, Part 2, Chap. 7

"We have him, Watson, we have him, and I dare swear that before to-morrow night he will be fluttering in our net as helpless as one of his own butterflies. A pin, a cork, and a card, and we add him to the Baker Street collection!" He burst into one of his rare fits of laughter as he turned away from the picture. I have not heard him laugh often, and it has always boded ill to somebody.

Holmes to Watson, on Stapleton,
The Hound of the Baskervilles, Chap. 13

Holmes, who loathed every form of society with his whole Bohemian soul, remained in our lodgings in Baker Street, buried among his old books, and alternating from week to week between cocaine and ambition, the drowsiness of the drug, and the fierce energy of his own keen nature.

Watson on Holmes,
A Scandal in Bohemia

"Try the settee," said Holmes, relapsing into his armchair and putting his fingertips together, as was his custom when in judicial moods.

Watson on Holmes,
The Red-Headed League

He curled himself up in his chair, with his thin knees drawn up to his hawk-like nose, and there he sat with his eyes closed and his black clay pipe thrusting out like the bill of some strange bird. I had come to the conclusion that he had dropped asleep, and indeed was nodding myself, when he suddenly sprang out of his chair with the gesture of a man who has made up his mind and put his pipe down upon the mantelpiece.

Watson on Holmes,
The Red-Headed League

All the afternoon he sat in the stalls wrapped in the most perfect happiness, gently waving his long, thin fingers in time to the music, while his gently smiling face and his languid, dreamy eyes were as unlike those of Holmes, the sleuth-hound, Holmes the relentless, keen-witted, ready-handed criminal agent, as it was possible to conceive.

Watson on Holmes,
The Red-Headed League

In his singular character the dual nature alternately asserted itself, and his extreme exactness and astuteness represented, as I have often thought, the reaction against the poetic and contemplative mood which occasionally predominated in him.

Watson on Holmes,
The Red-Headed League

The swing of his nature took him from extreme languor to devouring energy; and, as I knew well, he was never so truly formidable as when, for days on end, he had been lounging in his armchair amid his improvisations and his black-letter editions. Then it was that the lust of the chase would suddenly come upon him, and that his brilliant reasoning power would rise to the level of intuition, until those who were unacquainted with his methods would look askance at him as on a man whose knowledge was not that of other mortals.

Watson on Holmes,
The Red-Headed League

Sherlock Holmes sat silent for a few minutes with his fingertips still pressed together, his legs stretched out in front of him, and his gaze directed upward to the ceiling. Then he took down from the rack the old and oily clay pipe, which was to him as a counsellor, and, having lit it, he leaned back in his chair, with the thick blue cloud-wreaths spinning up from him, and a look of infinite languor in his face.

Watson on Holmes,
A Case of Identity

Sherlock Holmes was a man, however, who, when he had an unsolved problem upon his mind, would go for days, and even for a week, without rest, turning it over, rearranging his facts, looking at it from every point of view until he had either fathomed it or convinced himself that his data were insufficient.

Watson on Holmes,
The Man with the Twisted Lip

My companion sat in the front of the trap, his arms folded, his hat pulled down over his eyes, and his chin sunk upon his breast, buried in the deepest thought.

Watson on Holmes,
The Speckled Band

All that day and the next and the next Holmes was in a mood which his friends would call taciturn, and others morose. He ran out and ran in, smoked incessantly, played snatches on his violin, sank into reveries, devoured sandwiches at irregular hours, and hardly answered the casual questions which I put to him.

Watson on Holmes,
The Second Stain

He was bright, eager, and in excellent spirits, a mood which in his case alternated with fits of the blackest depression.

Watson on Holmes,
The Sign of Four, Chap. 3

There was that in the cool, nonchalant air of my companion which made him the last man with whom one would care to take anything approaching to a liberty.

Watson on Holmes,
The Sign of Four, Chap. 1

"I was never a very sociable fellow, Watson, always rather fond of moping in my rooms and working out my own little methods of thought."

Holmes to Watson,
The "Gloria Scott"

"It takes some imagination ..."

"See the value of imagination," said Holmes. "It is the one quality which Gregory lacks."

Holmes to Watson, on Insp. Gregory,
Silver Blaze

"You'll get results, Inspector, by always putting yourself in the other fellow's place, and thinking what you would do yourself. It takes some imagination, but it pays."

Holmes to Insp. MacKinnon,
The Retired Colourman

"When you have eliminated the impossible ..."

"How often have I said to you that when you have eliminated the impossible, whatever remains, however improbable, must be the truth?"

Holmes to Watson,
The Sign of Four, Chap. 6

"It is an old maxim of mine that when you have excluded the impossible, whatever remains, however improbable, must be the truth."

Holmes to Alexander Holder,
The Beryl Coronet

"Eliminate all other factors, and the one which remains must be the truth."

Holmes to Watson,
The Sign of Four, Chap. 1

"We must fall back upon the old axiom that when all other contingencies fail, whatever remains, however improbable, must be the truth."

Holmes to Watson,
The Bruce-Partington Plans

"That process," said I, "starts upon the supposition that when you have eliminated all which is impossible, then whatever remains, however improbable, must be the truth."

Holmes to Col. and Mrs. Emsworth,
The Blanched Soldier

"Just see how it glints and sparkles."

"It's a bonny thing," said he. "Just see how it glints and sparkles. Of course it is a nucleus and focus of crime. Every good stone is. They are the devil's pet baits. In the larger and older jewels every facet may stand for a bloody deed."

Holmes to Watson,
The Blue Carbuncle

"I am the last court of appeal."

"Let us see if there is justice upon the earth, or if we are ruled by chance."

Jefferson Hope,
A Study in Scarlet, Part 2, Chap. 6

A higher Judge had taken the matter in hand.

Watson,
A Study in Scarlet, Part 2, Chap. 7

"I am the last court of appeal."

Holmes to John Openshaw,
The Five Orange Pips

"After all, Watson," said Holmes, reaching up his hand for his clay pipe, "I am not retained by the police to supply their deficiencies. … I suppose that I am commuting a felony, but it is just possible that I am saving a soul. This fellow will not go wrong again; he is too terribly frightened. Send him to jail now, and you make him a jail-bird for life."

Holmes to Watson on James Ryder,
The Blue Carbuncle

"I am the last and highest court of appeal in detection."

Holmes to Watson,
The Sign of Four, Chap. 1

"I go into a case to help the ends of justice and the work of the police."

Holmes to White Mason,
The Valley of Fear, Part 1, Chap. 4

"I am generally recognized both by the public and by the official force as being a final court of appeal in doubtful cases."

Holmes to Watson,
The Musgrave Ritual

"My God! Are you in the police yourself?"
"No."
"What business is it of yours, then?"
"It's every man's business to see justice done."

Henry Wood and Holmes,
The Crooked Man

"All my instincts are one way, and all the facts are the other, and I much fear that British juries have not yet attained that pitch of intelligence when they will give the preference to my theories over Lestrade's facts."

Holmes to Watson,
The Norwood Builder

"Once or twice in my career I feel that I have done more real harm by my discovery of the criminal than ever he had done by his crime. I have learned caution now, and I had rather play tricks with the law of England than with my own conscience."

Holmes to Watson,
The Abbey Grange

"Watson, you are a British jury, and I never met a man who was more eminently fitted to represent one."

Holmes to Watson,
The Abbey Grange

Sherlock Holmes was threatened with prosecution for burglary, but when an object is good and a client is sufficiently illustrious, even the rigid British law becomes human and elastic.

Watson,
The Illustrious Client

"Human nature is a strange mixture, Watson."

"There is nothing new under the sun. It has all been done before."

Holmes to Insp. Gregson,
A Study in Scarlet, Part 1, Chap. 3

"For strange effects and extraordinary combinations we must go to life itself, which is always far more daring than any effort of the imagination."

Holmes to Watson,
The Red-Headed League

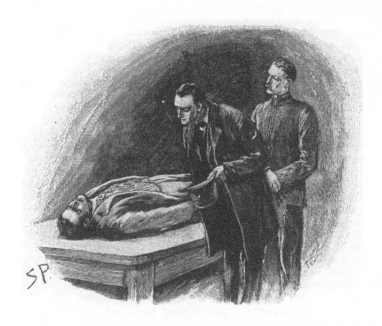

"My dear fellow," said Sherlock Holmes as we sat on either side of the fire in his lodgings at Baker Street, "life is infinitely stranger than anything which the mind of man could invent. We would not dare to conceive the things which are really mere commonplaces of existence. If we could fly out of that window hand in hand, hover over this great city, gently remove the roofs, and peep in at the queer things which are going on, the strange coincidences, the plannings, the cross-purposes, the wonderful chains of events, working through generations, and leading to the most outré results, it would make all fiction with its conventionalities and foreseen conclusions most stale and unprofitable."

Holmes to Watson,
A Case of Identity

"What is the meaning of it all, Mr. Holmes?"
"Ah, I have no data. I cannot tell."

Violet Hunter and Holmes,
The Copper Beeches

"Human nature is a strange mixture, Watson."

Holmes to Watson,
The Stock-Broker's Clerk

Sherlock Holmes was rubbing his hands and chuckling as he added this bizarre incident to his collection of strange episodes.

Watson on Holmes,
Wisteria Lodge

"Life is full of whimsical happenings, Watson."

Holmes to Watson,
The Mazarin Stone

"But there are always some lunatics about. It would be a dull world without them."

Holmes to Mary Maberley,
The Three Gables

"I naturally gravitated to London ..."

I naturally gravitated to London, that great cesspool into which all the loungers and idlers of the Empire are irresistibly drained.

Watson,
A Study in Scarlet, Part 1, Chap. 1

The sight of a friendly face in the great wilderness of London is a pleasant thing indeed to a lonely man.

Watson,
A Study in Scarlet, Part 1, Chap. 1

"I reckon that of all the mazes that ever were contrived, this city is the most confusing."

Jefferson Hope, on London,
A Study in Scarlet, Part 2, Chap. 6

"The air of London is the sweeter for my presence. In over a thousand cases I am not aware that I have ever used my powers upon the wrong side."

Holmes to Watson,
The Final Problem

Holmes's knowledge of the byways of London was extraordinary, and on this occasion he passed rapidly and with an assured step through a network of mews and stables, the very existence of which I had never known.

Holmes to Watson,
The Empty House

"Once again Mr. Sherlock Holmes is free to devote his life to examining those interesting little problems which the complex life of London so plentifully presents."

Holmes to Watson,
The Empty House

"From the point of view of the criminal expert," said Mr. Sherlock Holmes, "London has become a singularly uninteresting city since the death of the late lamented Professor Moriarty."

Holmes to Watson,
The Norwood Builder

In rapid succession we passed through the fringe of fashionable London, hotel London, theatrical London, literary London, commercial London, and, finally, maritime London, till we came to a riverside city of a hundred thousand souls, where the tenement houses swelter and reek with the outcasts of Europe.

Watson,
The Six Napoleons

"... one of those awful gray London castles which would make a church seem frivolous."

Watson,
The Illustrious Client

It was in the latter days of September, and the equinoctial gales had set in with exceptional violence. All day the wind had screamed and the rain had beaten against the windows, so that even here in the heart of great, hand-made London we were forced to raise our minds for the instant from the routine of life and to recognize the presence of those great elemental forces which shriek at mankind through the bars of his civilization, like untamed beasts in a cage.

Watson,
The Five Orange Pips

As to my companion, neither the country nor the sea presented the slightest attraction to him. He loved to lie in the very centre of five millions of people, with his filaments stretching out and running through them, responsive to every little rumour or suspicion of unsolved crime.

Watson on Holmes,
The Resident Patient

For three hours we strolled about together, watching the ever-changing kaleidoscope of life as it ebbs and flows through Fleet Street and the Strand.

Watson,
The Resident Patient

"He never spoke of the softer passions ..."

All emotions, and that one particularly, were abhorrent to his cold, precise but admirably balanced mind. He was, I take it, the most perfect reasoning and observing machine that the world has seen, but as a lover he would have placed himself in a false position. He never spoke of the softer passions, save with a gibe and a sneer.

Watson on Holmes's attitude to love,
A Scandal in Bohemia

But for the trained reasoner to admit such intrusions into his own delicate and finely adjusted temperament was to introduce a distracting factor which might throw a doubt upon all his mental results. Grit in a sensitive instrument, or a crack in one of his own high-power lenses, would not be more disturbing than a strong emotion in a nature such as his.

Watson on Holmes,
A Scandal in Bohemia

"We can't command our love, but we can our actions."
Hattie Doran (Mrs. Francis Hay Moulton),
The Noble Bachelor

"It is of the first importance," he cried, "not to allow your judgment to be biased by personal qualities. A client is to me a mere unit, a factor in a problem. The emotional qualities are antagonistic to clear reasoning."

Holmes to Watson,
The Sign of Four, Chap. 2

"But love is an emotional thing, and whatever is emotional is opposed to that true cold reason which I place above all things. I should never marry myself, lest I bias my judgment."

Holmes to Watson,
The Sign of Four, Chap. 12

"Jealousy is a strange transformer of characters."
Holmes to Lord St. Simon,
The Noble Bachelor

"Of all ghosts the ghosts of our old loves are the worst."
Justice Trevor to Holmes,
The "Gloria Scott"

"A man always finds it hard to realize that he may have finally lost a woman's love, however badly he may have treated her."

Holmes to Watson,
The Musgrave Ritual

"Work is the best antidote to sorrow, my dear Watson."
Holmes to Watson,
The Empty House

"The features are given to man as the means by which he shall express his emotions, and yours are faithful servants."

Holmes to Watson,
The Resident Patient

Sometimes I found myself regarding him as an isolated phenomenon, a brain without a heart, as deficient in human sympathy as he was preeminent in intelligence.

Watson on Holmes,
The Greek Interpreter

"It is part of the settled order of Nature that such a girl should have followers," said Holmes, as he pulled at his meditative pipe, "but for choice not on bicycles in lonely country roads."

Holmes to Watson,
The Solitary Cyclist

"Well," said Lestrade, "I've seen you handle a good many cases, Mr. Holmes, but I don't know that I ever knew a more workmanlike one than that. We're not jealous of you at Scotland Yard. No, sir, we are very proud of you, and if you come down to-morrow, there's not a man, from the oldest inspector to the youngest constable, who wouldn't be glad to shake you by the hand."

"Thank you!" said Holmes. "Thank you!" and as he turned away, it seemed to me that he was more nearly moved by the softer human emotions than I had ever seen him.

Insp. Lestrade and Holmes,
The Six Napoleons

"I am not often eloquent. I use my head, not my heart."

Holmes to Watson,
The Illustrious Client

"I have never loved, Watson, but if I did and if the woman I loved had met such an end, I might act even as our lawless lion-hunter has done. Who knows?"

Holmes to Watson,
The Devil's Foot

"You would not call me a marrying man, Watson?"

"Ah, Watson," said Holmes, smiling, "perhaps you would not be
very gracious either, if, after all the trouble of wooing and wedding,
you found yourself deprived in an instant of wife and of fortune."

Holmes to Watson,
The Noble Bachelor

"You would not call me a marrying man, Watson?"
"No, indeed!"
"You'll be interested to hear that I'm engaged."
"My dear fellow! I congrat –"
"To Milverton's housemaid."
"Good heavens, Holmes!"
"I wanted information, Watson."
"Surely you have gone too far?"
"It was a most necessary step. I am a plumber with a rising busi-
ness, Escott, by name. I have walked out with her each evening, and I
have talked with her. Good heavens, those talks! However, I have got
all I wanted. I know Milverton's house as I know the palm of my hand."
"But the girl, Holmes?"
He shrugged his shoulders.

"You can't help it, my dear Watson. You must play your cards as best you can when such a stake is on the table."

Holmes and Watson,
Charles Augustus Milverton

"It is a pity he did not write in pencil," said he, throwing them down again with a shrug of disappointment. "As you have no doubt frequently observed, Watson, the impression usually goes through – a fact which has dissolved many a happy marriage."

Holmes to Watson,
The Missing Three-Quarter

The good Watson had at that time deserted me for a wife, the only selfish action which I can recall in our association.

Holmes on Watson,
The Blanched Soldier

"You know my methods."

"You know my methods. Apply them!"

Holmes to Watson,
The Hound of the Baskervilles, Chap. 1

"It is a singular thing, but I find that a concentrated atmosphere helps a concentration of thought. I have not pushed it to the length of getting into a box to think, but that is the logical outcome of my convictions."

Holmes to Watson,
The Hound of the Baskervilles, Chap. 3

"I thought that you were in Baker Street working out that case of blackmailing."

"That was what I wished you to think."

"Then you use me, and yet do not trust me!" I cried with some bitterness. "I think that I have deserved better at your hands, Holmes."

"My dear fellow, you have been invaluable to me in this as in many other cases, and I beg that you will forgive me if I have seemed to play a trick upon you."

Watson and Holmes,
The Hound of the Baskervilles, Chap. 12

"He has his own little methods, which are, if he won't mind my saying so, just a little too theoretical and fantastic, but he has the makings of a detective in him.

Peter Jones of Scotland Yard on Holmes,
The Red-Headed League

"You know my method. It is founded upon the observation of trifles."

Holmes to Watson,
Boscombe Valley

"I wish I knew how you reach your results."
"I reached this one," said my friend, "by sitting upon five pillows and consuming an ounce of shag."

Watson and Holmes,
The Man with the Twisted Lip

"Here is my lens. You know my methods. What can you gather yourself as to the individuality of the man who has worn this article?"

Holmes to Watson,
The Blue Carbuncle

"I never make exceptions. An exception disproves the rule."

Holmes to Watson,
The Sign of Four, Chap. 2

"My dear Watson, try a little analysis yourself," said he with a touch of impatience. "You know my methods. Apply them, and it will be instructive to compare results."

Holmes to Watson,
The Sign of Four, Chap. 6

"Nothing clears up a case so much as stating it to another person."

Holmes to Watson,
Silver Blaze

"I follow my own methods and tell as much or as little as I choose. That is the advantage of being unofficial."

Holmes to Watson,
Silver Blaze

"My dear fellow, you know my methods."

Holmes to Watson,
The Stock-Broker's Clerk

"Well, we have seen some very interesting things. I'll tell you what we did as we walk. First of all, we saw the body of this unfortunate man. He certainly died from a revolver wound as reported."

"Had you doubted it, then?"

"Oh, it is as well to test everything."

Holmes and Watson,
The Reigate Puzzle

"I am afraid that my explanation may disillusion you, but it has always been my habit to hide none of my methods, either from my friend Watson or from anyone who might take an intelligent interest in them."

Holmes to Col. Hayter,
The Reigate Puzzle

"You know my methods, Watson."

Holmes to Watson,
The Crooked Man

"One should always look for a possible alternative, and provide against it. It is the first rule of criminal investigation."

Holmes to Watson,
Black Peter

"Well, well, you have your own methods, Mr. Sherlock Holmes, and it is not for me to say a word against them, but I think I have done a better day's work than you."

Insp. Lestrade to Holmes,
The Six Napoleons

"You know my methods in such cases, Watson. I put myself in the man's place, and, having first gauged his intelligence, I try to imagine how I should myself have proceeded under the same circumstances."

Holmes to Watson,
The Musgrave Ritual

"I cannot live without brainwork."

"What one man can invent another can discover."

Holmes to Abe Slaney,
The Dancing Men

I knew by experience that my companion's brain was so abnormally active that it was dangerous to leave it without material upon which to work.

Watson on Holmes,
The Missing Three-Quarter

"My mind," he said, "rebels at stagnation. Give me problems, give me work, give me the most abstruse cryptogram, or the most intricate analysis, and I am in my own proper atmosphere. I can dispense then with artificial stimulants. But I abhor the dull routine of existence. I crave for mental exaltation. That is why I have chosen my own particular profession, or rather created it, for I am the only one in the world."

Holmes to Watson,
The Sign of Four, Chap. 1

"I cannot live without brainwork. What else is there to live for?"

Holmes to Watson,
The Sign of Four, Chap. 1

"As I focus my mind upon it, it seems rather less impenetrable."
Holmes to Watson,
The Valley of Fear, Part 1, Chap. 1

"My dear Watson, you know how bored I have been since we locked up Colonel Carruthers. My mind is like a racing engine, tearing itself to pieces because it is not connected up with the work for which it was built. Life is commonplace; the papers are sterile; audacity and romance seem to have passed forever from the criminal world. Can you ask me, then, whether I am ready to look into any new problem, however trivial it may prove?"
Holmes to Watson,
Wisteria Lodge

One of the most remarkable characteristics of Sherlock Holmes was his power of throwing his brain out of action and switching all his thoughts on to lighter things whenever he had convinced himself that he could no longer work to advantage. I remember that during the whole of that memorable day he lost himself in a monograph which he had undertaken upon the Polyphonic Motets of Lassus.
Watson on Holmes,
The Bruce-Partington Plans

"But why not eat?"
"Because the faculties become refined when you starve them. Why, surely, as a doctor, my dear Watson, you must admit that what your digestion gains in the way of blood supply is so much lost to the brain."
Watson and Holmes,
The Mazarin Stone

"To let the brain work without sufficient material is like racing an engine. It racks itself to pieces."
Holmes to Watson,
The Devil's Foot

"Behold the fruit of pensive nights and laborious days."
Holmes to Watson, on his book about bees,
His Last Bow

"I make a blunder ..."

"I am afraid, my dear Watson, that most of your conclusions were erroneous. When I said that you stimulated me I meant, to be frank, that in noting your fallacies I was occasionally guided towards the truth."

Holmes to Watson,
The Hound of the Baskervilles, Chap. 1

So accustomed was I to his invariable success that the very possibility of his failing had ceased to enter into my head.

Watson on Holmes,
A Scandal in Bohemia

"We have certainly been favoured with extraordinary luck during this inquiry, and it will be entirely our own fault if we do not succeed in clearing the matter up."

Holmes to Watson,
The Beryl Coronet

"I have been beaten four times – three times by men, and once by a woman."

Holmes to John Openshaw,
The Five Orange Pips

"I think, Watson, that you are now standing in the presence of one of the most absolute fools in Europe. I deserve to be kicked from here to Charing Cross."

Holmes to Watson,
The Man with the Twisted Lip

"I confess that I have been as blind as a mole, but it is better to learn wisdom late than never to learn it at all."

Holmes to Watson,
The Man with the Twisted Lip

"I am afraid, Holmes, that you are not very practical with your deductions and your inferences. You have made two blunders in as many minutes."

Insp. Lestrade to Holmes,
The Noble Bachelor

"Ah, that is good luck. I could only say what was the balance of probability. I did not at all expect to be so accurate."

Holmes to Watson,
The Sign of Four, Chap. 1

He was likely, I thought, to fall into error through the over-refinement of his logic — his preference for a subtle and bizarre explanation when a plainer and more commonplace one lay ready to his hand.

Watson on Holmes,
The Sign of Four, Chap. 9

"I made a blunder, my dear Watson – which is, I am afraid, a more common occurrence than anyone would think who only knew me through your memoirs."

Holmes to Watson,
Silver Blaze

"I assure you it is just as hateful to me to fail in a case as it can be to you to blunder over a commission."

Holmes to Percy Phelps,
The Naval Treaty

"Should you care to add the case to your annals, my dear Watson," said Holmes that evening, "it can only be as an example of that temporary eclipse to which even the best-balanced mind may be exposed. Such slips are common to all mortals, and the greatest is he who can recognize and repair them. To this modified credit I may, perhaps, make some claim."

Holmes to Watson,
Lady Francis Carfax

... the scarlet thread of murder ..."

"There's the scarlet thread of murder running through the colourless skein of life, and our duty is to unravel it, and isolate it, and expose every inch of it."

Holmes to Watson,
A Study in Scarlet, Part 1, Chap. 4

"A very commonplace little murder."

Holmes to Watson,
The Naval Treaty

"... off to violin-land ..."

"A well-played violin is a treat for the gods – a badly played one –"

Watson to Holmes,
A Study in Scarlet, Part 1, Chap. 1

"Do you remember what Darwin says about music? He claims that the power of producing and appreciating it existed among the human race long before the power of speech was arrived at. Perhaps that is why we are so subtly influenced by it. There are vague memories in our souls of those misty centuries when the world was in its childhood."

Holmes to Watson,
A Study in Scarlet, Part 1, Chap. 5

"I observe that there is a good deal of German music on the programme, which is rather more to my taste than Italian or French. It is introspective, and I want to introspect."

Holmes to Watson,
The Red-Headed League

And now, Doctor, we've done our work, so it's time we had some play. A sandwich and a cup of coffee, and then off to violinland, where all is sweetness and delicacy and harmony."

Holmes to Watson,
The Red-Headed League

My friend was an enthusiastic musician, being himself not only a very capable performer but a composer of no ordinary merit.

Watson on Holmes,
The Red-Headed League

Leaning back in his armchair of an evening, he would close his eyes and scrape carelessly at the fiddle which was thrown across his knee.

Watson on Holmes,
A Study in Scarlet, Part 1, Chapt. 1

And now, Doctor, we've done our work, so it's time we had some play. A sandwich and a cup of coffee, and then off to violin-land, where all is sweetness and delicacy and harmony."

Holmes to Watson,
The Red-Headed League

He took up his violin from the corner, and as I stretched myself out he began to play some low, dreamy, melodious air –his own, no doubt, for he had a remarkable gift for improvisation.

Watson on Holmes,
The Sign of Four, Chap. 8

"Brother Mycroft is coming round."

"Well, well! What next?" said he. "Brother Mycroft is coming round."

"Why not?" I asked.

"Why not? It is as if you met a tram-car coming down a country lane. Mycroft has his rails and he runs on them. His Pall Mall lodgings, the Diogenes Club, Whitehall — that is his cycle. Once, and only once, he has been here. What upheaval can possibly have derailed him?"

Holmes and Watson,
The Bruce-Partington Plans

"He has the tidiest and most orderly brain, with the greatest capacity for storing facts, of any man living. The same great powers which I have turned to the detection of crime he has used for this particular business. The conclusions of every department are passed to him, and he is the central exchange, the clearing-house, which makes out the balance. All other men are specialists, but his specialism is omniscience."

Holmes on Mycroft Holmes,
The Bruce-Partington Plans

A moment later the tall and portly form of Mycroft Holmes was ushered into the room. Heavily built and massive, there was a suggestion of uncouth physical inertia in the figure, but above this unwieldy frame there was perched a head so masterful in its brow, so alert in its steel-gray, deep-set eyes, so firm in its lips, and so subtle in its play of expression, that after the first glance one forgot the gross body and remembered only the dominant mind.

Watson on Mycroft Holmes,
The Bruce-Partington Plans

"There is a mystery about this ..."

"There is a mystery about this which stimulates the imagination; where there is no imagination there is no horror."

Holmes to Watson,
A Study in Scarlet, Part 1, Chap. 5

"There is no great mystery in this matter," he said, taking the cup of tea which I had poured out for him; "the facts appear to admit of only one explanation."

Holmes to Watson,
The Sign of Four, Chap. 3

"I am sorry," said Holmes. "I am accustomed to have mystery at one end of my cases, but to have it at both ends is confusing."

Holmes to Sir James Damery,
The Illustrious Client

"How small we feel ..."

"One's ideas must be as broad as Nature if they are to interpret Nature."

Holmes to Watson,
A Study in Scarlet, Part 1, Chap. 5

"Observation with me is second nature."

Holmes to Watson,
A Study in Scarlet, Part 1, Chap.

"How small we feel with our petty ambitions and strivings in the presence of the great elemental forces of Nature!"

Holmes to Watson,
The Sign of Four, Chap. 7

Appreciation of nature found no place among his many gifts, and his only change was when he turned his mind from the evil-doer of the town to track down his brother of the country.

Watson on Holmes,
The Resident Patient

"You see, but you do not observe."

"I have a turn both for observation and for deduction."

Holmes to Watson
A Study in Scarlet, Part 1, Chap. 2

"There is a strong family resemblance about misdeeds, and if you have all the details of a thousand at your finger ends, it is odd if you can't unravel the thousand and first."

Holmes to Watson,
A Study in Scarlet, Part 1, Chap. 2

"The world is full of obvious things which nobody by any chance ever observes."

Holmes to Watson,
The Hound of the Baskervilles, Chap. 3

"My dear doctor, this is a time for observation, not for talk."

Holmes to Watson,
The Red-Headed League

"Perhaps I have trained myself to see what others overlook."

Holmes to Mary Sutherland,
A Case of Identity

"You see, but you do not observe. The distinction is clear."

Holmes to Watson,
A Scandal in Bohemia

"We approached the case, you remember, with an absolutely blank mind, which is always an advantage. We had formed no theories. We were simply there to observe and to draw inferences from our observations."

Holmes to Watson,
The Cardboard Box

"You see everything."
"I see no more than you, but I have trained myself to notice what I see."

James M. Dodd and Holmes,
The Blanched Soldier

"... the calculation is a simple one."

"You mentioned your name, as if I should recognize it,

but I assure you that, beyond the obvious facts that you are a bachelor, a solicitor, a Freemason, and an asthmatic, I know nothing whatever about you."

Holmes to John Hector McFarlane,
The Norwood Builder

"You know a conjurer gets no credit when once he has explained his trick and if I show you too much of my method of working, you will come to the conclusion that I am a very ordinary individual after all."

Holmes to Watson,
A Study in Scarlet, Part 1, Chap. 4

"Well, Watson, what do you make of it?"

Holmes was sitting with his back to me, and I had given him no sign of my occupation.

"How did you know what I was doing? I believe you have eyes in the back of your head."

"I have, at least, a well-polished, silver-plated coffeepot in front of me," said he.

Holmes and Watson,
The Hound of the Baskervilles, Chap. 1

"Beyond the obvious facts that he has at some time done manual labour, that he takes snuff, that he is a Freemason, that he has been in China, and that he has done a considerable amount of writing lately, I can deduce nothing else."

Holmes on Jabez Wilson,
The Red-Headed League

"I am a dangerous man to fall foul of! See here." He stepped swiftly forward, seized the poker, and bent it into a curve with his huge brown hands.

"See that you keep yourself out of my grip," he snarled, and hurling the twisted poker into the fireplace he strode out of the room.

"He seems a very amiable person," said Holmes, laughing.

"I am not quite so bulky, but if he had remained I might have shown him that my grip was not much more feeble than his own." As he spoke he picked up the steel poker and, with a sudden effort, straightened it out again.

Dr. Grimseby Roylott and Holmes,
The Speckled Band

"We are going well," said he, looking out of the window and glancing at his watch. "Our rate at present is fifty-three and a half miles an hour."

"I have not observed the quarter-mile posts," said I.

"Nor have I. But the telegraph posts upon this line are sixty yards apart, and the calculation is a simple one."

Holmes and Watson,
Silver Blaze

"I am afraid that I rather give myself away when I explain." said he. "Results without causes are much more impressive."

Holmes to Watson,
The Stock-Broker's Clerk

"You see, my dear Watson" – he propped his test-tube in the rack, and began to lecture with the air of a professor addressing his class – "it is not really difficult to construct a series of inferences, each dependent upon its predecessor and each simple in itself. If, after doing so, one simply knocks out all the central inferences and presents one's audience with the starting-point and the conclusion, one may produce a startling, though possibly a meretricious, effect."

Holmes to Watson,
The Dancing Men

"You know my powers ..."

"You know my powers, my dear Watson."

Holmes to Watson,
The Final Problem

"I believe that you are a wizard, Mr. Holmes. I really do sometimes think that you have powers that are not human."

> Insp. Stanley Hopkins to Holmes,
> *The Abbey Grange*

"What is the use of having powers, Doctor, when one has no field upon which to exert them?"

> Holmes to Watson,
> *The Sign of Four*, Chap. 1

"What a chorus of groans, cries, and bleatings!"

"The Press, Watson, is a most valuable institution, if you only know how to use it."

> Holmes to Watson,
> *The Six Napoleons*

He took down the great book in which, day by day, he filed the agony columns of the various London journals.

"Dear me!" said he, turning over the pages, "what a chorus of groans, cries, and bleatings! What a rag-bag of singular happenings! But surely the most valuable hunting ground that ever was given to a student of the unusual!"

> Watson on Holmes,
> *The Red Circle*

"I read nothing except the criminal news and the agony column. The latter is always instructive."

> Holmes to Watson,
> *The Noble Bachelor*

"Nothing of interest in the paper, Watson?" he said.

I was aware that by anything of interest, Holmes meant anything of criminal interest. There was the news of a revolution, of a possible war, and of an impending change of government; but these did not come within the horizon of my companion.

> Holmes and Watson,
> *The Bruce-Partington Plans*

"It is a very sweet little problem ..."

"Draw your chair up and hand me my violin, for the only problem we have still to solve is how to while away these bleak autumnal evenings."

Holmes to Watson,
The Noble Bachelor

"It may turn out to be of more interest than you think. You remember that the affair of the blue carbuncle, which appeared to be a mere whim at first, developed into a serious investigation."

Watson to Holmes,
The Copper Beeches

"It is a very sweet little problem, and I would not have missed it for a good deal."

Holmes to Watson,
The Beryl Coronet

"Oh, you may carry that feeling away with you. I assure you that your little problem promises to be the most interesting which has come my way for some months. There is something distinctly novel about some of the features."

Holmes to Violent Hunter,
The Copper Beeches

"It is a case, Watson, which may prove to have something in it, or may prove to have nothing, but which, at least, presents those unusual and outré features which are as dear to you as they are to me."

Holmes to Watson,
The Stock-Broker's Clerk

"They are not all successes, Watson," said he. "But there are some pretty little problems among them."

Holmes to Watson,
The Musgrave Ritual

"Once again Mr. Sherlock Holmes is free to devote his life to examining those interesting little problems which the complex life of London so plentifully presents."

Holmes to Watson,
The Empty House

"Every problem becomes very childish when once it is explained to you."

Holmes to Watson,
The Dancing Men

"Although it is trivial, it is undoubtedly queer, and I know that you have a taste for all that is out of the common."

Insp. Lestrade to Holmes,
The Six Napoleons

"I should prefer that you do not mention my name at all in connection with the case, as I choose to be only associated with those crimes which present some difficulty in their solution."

Holmes to Insp. Lestrade,
The Cardboard Box

"It is quite a three pipe problem ..."

"Nonetheless, you must come round to my view, for otherwise I shall keep on piling fact upon fact on you until your reason breaks down under them and acknowledges me to be right."

Holmes to Watson,
The Red-Headed League

"What are you going to do, then?" I asked.
"To smoke," he answered. "It is quite a three pipe problem, and I beg that you won't speak to me for fifty minutes."

Watson and Holmes,
The Red-Headed League

Here I had heard what he had heard, I had seen what he had seen, and yet from his words it was evident that he saw clearly not only what had happened but what was about to happen, while to me the whole business was still confused and grotesque.

Watson on Holmes,
The Red-Headed League

"You reasoned it out beautifully," I exclaimed in unfeigned admiration. "It is so long a chain, and yet every link rings true." "It saved me from ennui," he answered, yawning.

Watson and Holmes,
The Red-Headed League

" 'Pon my word, Watson, you are coming along wonderfully. You have really done very well indeed. It is true that you have missed everything of importance, but you have hit upon the method, and you have a quick eye for colour. Never trust to general impressions, my boy, but concentrate yourself upon details. My first glance is always at a woman's sleeve. In a man it is perhaps better first to take the knee of the trouser."

Holmes to Watson,
A Case of Identity

I had had so many reasons to believe in my friend's subtle powers of reasoning and extraordinary energy in action that I felt that he must have some solid grounds for the assured and easy demeanour with which he treated the singular mystery which he had been called upon to fathom.

Watson on Holmes,
A Case of Identity

"It seems absurdly simple, and yet, somehow I can get nothing to go upon. There's plenty of thread, no doubt, but I can't get the end of it into my hand."

Holmes to Watson,
The Man with the Twisted Lip

"I have no doubt that I am very stupid, but I must confess that I am unable to follow you."

Watson to Holmes,
The Blue Carbuncle

"Circumstantial evidence is a very tricky thing," answered Holmes thoughtfully. "It may seem to point very straight to one thing, but if you shift your own point of view a little, you may find it pointing in an equally uncompromising manner to something entirely different."

Holmes to Watson,
Boscombe Valley

"I have almost every link in my hands, and all the proofs which I could possibly need, so there is little which you need tell me. Still, that little may as well be cleared up to make the case complete."

Holmes to James Ryder,
The Blue Carbuncle

I had no keener pleasure than in following Holmes in his professional investigations, and in admiring the rapid deductions, as swift as intuitions, and yet always founded on a logical basis with which he unravelled the problems which were submitted to him.

Watson on Holmes,
The Speckled Band

"My whole examination served to turn my conjecture into a certainty. Circumstantial evidence is occasionally very convincing, as when you find a trout in the milk, to quote Thoreau's example."

Holmes to Watson,
The Noble Bachelor

"Though unsatisfactory, my research has not been entirely barren."

Holmes to Watson,
The Sign of Four, Chap. 1

"I never guess. It is a shocking habit – destructive to the logical faculty."

Holmes to Watson,
The Sign of Four, Chap. 1

"There, Watson! What do you think of pure reason and its fruit?"

Holmes to Watson,
The Valley of Fear, Part 1, Chap. 1

"Ah! my dear Watson, there we come into those realms of conjecture, where the most logical mind may be at fault."

Holmes to Watson,
The Empty House

There was something in the ice-cold reasoning of Holmes which made it impossible to shrink from any adventure which he might recommend.

Watson on Holmes,
Wisteria Lodge

"The train of reasoning is not very obscure, Watson," said Holmes with a mischievous twinkle.

Holmes to Watson,
Lady Francis Carfax

"Let us consider the problem in the light of pure reason."

Holmes to Watson,
The Valley of Fear, Part 1, Chap. 1

"Well, Watson, I will not offend your intelligence by explaining what is obvious."

Holmes to Watson,
The Devil's Foo

Our official detectives ...

"Gregson is the smartest of the Scotland Yarders," my

friend remarked; "he and Lestrade are the pick of a bad lot."
Holmes to Watson,
A Study in Scarlet, Part 1, Chap. 3

"He is not a bad fellow, though an absolute imbecile in his profession. He has one positive virtue. He is as brave as a bulldog and as tenacious as a lobster if he gets his claws upon anyone."
Holmes on Peter Jones of Scotland Yard,
The Red-Headed League

In recording from time to time some of the curious experiences and interesting recollections which I associate with my long and intimate friendship with Mr. Sherlock Holmes, I have continually been faced by difficulties caused by his own aversion to publicity. To his sombre and cynical spirit all popular applause was always abhorrent, and nothing amused him more at the end of a successful case than to hand over the actual exsposure to to some orthodox official, and to listen with a mocking smile to the general chorus of misplaced congratulation.

Watson on Holmes,
The Devil's Foot

"I am a man of somewhat retiring, and I might even say refined, tastes, and there is nothing more unaesthetic than a policeman."

Thaddeus Sholto to Holmes and Watson,
The Sign of Four, Chap. 4

"I'll do you this justice, Mr. Holmes, that I was never in a case yet that I didn't feel stronger for having you on my side."

Insp. Gregson to Holmes,
The Red Circle

Our official detectives may blunder in the matter of intelligence, but never in that of courage.

Watson on Insp. Gregson,
The Red Circle

"Besides, on general principles it is best that I should not leave the country. Scotland Yard feels lonely without me, and it causes an unhealthy excitement among the criminal classes."

Holmes to Watson,
Lady Francis Carfax

"There may be an occasional want of imagination down there, but they lead the world for thoroughness and method."

Holmes to Watson, on Scotland Yard,
The Three Garridebs

"It is simplicity itself ..."

"Simple as it was, there were several most instructive points about it."

Holmes to Watson,
A Study in Scarlet, Part 2, Chap. 7

"The proof of its intrinsic simplicity is, that without any help save a few very ordinary deductions I was able to lay my hand upon the criminal within three days."

Holmes to Watson,
A Study in Scarlet, Part 2, Chap. 7

"The case has been an interesting one," remarked Holmes when our visitors had left us, "because it serves to show very clearly how simple the explanation may be of an affair which at first sight seems to be almost inexplicable."

Holmes to Watson,
The Noble Bachelor

"It is simplicity itself," he remarked, chuckling at my surprise – "so absurdly simple that an explanation is superfluous."

Holmes to Watson,
The Sign of Four, Chap. 1

"Pshaw, my dear boy! it was simplicity itself."

Holmes to Watson,
The Sign of Four, Chap. 7

"Perhaps, when a man has special knowledge and special powers like my own, it rather encourages him to seek a complex explanation when a simpler one is at hand."

Holmes to Insp Stanley Hopkins,
The Abbey Grange

"I have made a special study of cigar ashes ..."

"I have made a special study of cigar ashes – in fact, I have written a monograph upon the subject. I flatter myself that I can distinguish at a glance the ash of any known brand either of cigar or of tobacco.

Holmes to Watson,
A Study in Scarlet, Part 1, Chap. 4

89

"To the trained eye there is as much difference between the black ash of a Trichinopoly and the white fluff of bird's-eye as there is between a cabbage and a potato."

> Holmes to Watson, on tobacco ash,
> *The Sign of Four,* Chap. 1

"I trust that you have no objection to tobacco-smoke, to the balsamic odour of the Eastern tobacco. I am a little nervous, and I find my hookah an invaluable sedative."

> Thaddeus Sholto to Holmes and Watson,
> *The Sign of Four,* Chap. 4

"It is, of course, a trifle ..."

"You know my method. It is founded upon the observation of trifles."

> Holmes to Watson,
> *Boscombe Valley*

"The matter is a perfectly trivial one" – he jerked his thumb in the direction of the old hat – "but there are points in connection with it which are not entirely devoid of interest and even of instruction."

> Holmes to Watson,
> *The Blue Carbuncle*

"It has long been an axiom of mine that the little things are infinitely the most important."

> Holmes to Mary Sutherland,
> *A Case of Identity*

"It is, of course, a trifle, but there is nothing so important as trifles."

> Holmes to Mrs. Neville St. Clair,
> *The Man with the Twisted Lip*

"I am an omnivorous reader with a strangely retentive memory for trifles."

Holmes to Ian Murdoch,
The Lion's Mane

"I have no time for trifles."

Holmes to Watson,
A Study in Scarlet, Part 1, Chap. 3

No man burdens his mind with small matters unless he has some very good reason for doing so.

Watson on Holmes,
A Study in Scarlet, Part 1, Chap. 2

"The affair seems absurdly trifling, and yet I dare call nothing trivial when I reflect that some of my most classic cases have had the least promising commencement. You will remember, Watson, how the dreadful business of the Abernetty family was first brought to my notice by the depth which the parsley had sunk into the butter upon a hot day."

Holmes to Watson and Lestrade,
The Six Napoleons

"Any truth is better ..."

"Any truth is better than indefinite doubt."

Holmes to Grant Munro,
The Yellow Face

"My blushes, Watson!"

"This fellow may be very clever," I said to myself, "but he is certainly very conceited."

Watson on Holmes,
A Study in Scarlet, Part 1, Chap. 2

"You have heard me speak of Professor Moriarty?"

"The famous scientific criminal, as famous among crooks as — "

"My blushes, Watson!" Holmes murmured in a deprecating voice.

"I was about to say, as he is unknown to the public."

"A touch! A distinct touch!" cried Holmes. "You are developing a certain unexpected vein of pawky humour, Watson, against which I must learn to guard myself."

Holmes and Watson,
The Valley of Fear, Part 1, Chap. 1

He was always warmed by genuine admiration — the characteristic of the real artist.

Watson on Holmes,
The Valley of Fear, Part 1, Chap. 2

"Watson," said he, "if it should ever strike you that I am getting a little overconfident in my powers, or giving less pains to a case than it deserves, kindly whisper 'Norbury' in my ear, and I shall be infinitely obliged to you."

Holmes to Watson,
The Yellow Face

"My dear Watson," said he, "I cannot agree with those who rank modesty among the virtues. To the logician all things should be seen exactly as they are, and to underestimate one's self is as much a departure from truth as to exaggerate one's own powers."

Holmes to Watson,
The Greek Interpreter

Holmes was accessible upon the side of flattery, and also, to do him justice, upon the side of kindliness.

Watson on Holmes,
The Red Circle

"My poor little reputation, such as it is, will suffer shipwreck if I am so candid."

Holmes to Watson,
The Red-Headed League

"Every man finds his limitations, Mr. Holmes, but at least it cures us of the weakness of self-satisfaction.

Lord Cantlemere to Holmes,
The Mazarin Stone

"... vengeance would be sweet ..."

"There is no satisfaction in vengeance unless the offender has time to realize who it is that strikes him, and why retribution has come upon him."

Jefferson Hope,
A Study in Scarlet, Part 2, Chap. 6

"I had always known that vengeance would be sweet, but I had never hoped for the contentment of soul which now possessed me."

Jefferson Hope,
A Study in Scarlet, Part 2, Chap. 6

"Violence does, in truth, recoil upon the violent, and the schemer falls into the pit which he digs for another."

Holmes to Watson,
The Speckled Band

"I think there are certain crimes which the law cannot touch, and which therefore, to some extent, justify private revenge."

Holmes to Insp. Lestrade,
Charles Augustus Milverton

"To revenge crime is important, but to prevent it is more so."

Sir James Damery to Holmes,
The Illustrious Client

"Good old Watson!"

"Really, Watson, you excel yourself," said Holmes, pushing back his chair and lighting a cigarette. "I am bound to say that in all the accounts which you have been so good as to give of my own small achievements you have habitually underrated your own abilities. It may be that you are not yourself luminous, but you are a conductor of light. Some people without possessing genius have a remarkable power of stimulating it. I confess, my dear fellow, that I am very much in your debt."

Holmes to Watson,
The Hound of the Baskervilles, Chap. 1

"There is an appalling directness about your questions, Watson," said Holmes, shaking his pipe at me. "They come at me like bullets."

Holmes to Watson,
The Valley of Fear, Part 1, Chap. 6

"There is a delightful freshness about you, Watson, which makes it a pleasure to exercise any small powers which I possess at your expense."

> Holmes to Watson,
> *The Hound of the Baskervilles*, Chap. 3

"If my friend would undertake it there is no man who is better worth having at your side when you are in a tight place. No one can say so more confidently than I."

> Holmes on Watson,
> *The Hound of the Baskervilles*, Chap. 5

"My dear Watson, you were born to be a man of action. Your instinct is always to do something energetic."

> Holmes to Watson,
> *The Hound of the Baskervilles*, Chap. 13

I trust that I am not more dense than my neighbours, but I was always oppressed with a sense of my own stupidity in my dealings with Sherlock Holmes.

> Watson on himself,
> *The Red-Headed League*

"You have a grand gift of silence, Watson," said he. "It makes you quite invaluable as a companion.

> Holmes to Watson,
> *The Man with the Twisted Lip*

"You will realize that among your many talents dissimulation finds no place."

> Holmes to Watson,
> *The Dying Detective*

"Good old Watson!"

> Holmes to Watson,
> *The Illustrious Client*

"Good old Watson! You are the one fixed point in a changing age."

Holmes to Watson,
His Last Bow

The ideas of my friend Watson, though limited, are exceedingly pertinacious.

Holmes,
The Blanched Soldier

Speaking of my old friend and biographer, I would take this opportunity to remark that if I burden myself with a companion in my various little inquiries it is not done out of sentiment or caprice, but it is that Watson has some remarkable characteristics of his own to which in his modesty he has given small attention amid his exaggerated estimates of my own performances. A confederate who foresees your conclusions and course of action is always dangerous, but one to whom each development comes as a perpetual surprise, and to whom the future is always a closed book, is indeed an ideal helpmate.

Holmes on Watson,
The Blanched Soldier

"I never get your limits, Watson," said he. "There are unexplored possibilities about you."

Holmes to Watson,
The Sussex Vampire

"Now, Watson, the fair sex is your department."

"She was a lovely woman, with a face that a man might die for.

Holmes to Watson, on Irene Adler,
A Scandal in Bohemia

"I am not a whole-souled admirer of womankind, as you are aware, Watson, but my experience of life has taught me that there are few wives, having any regard for their husbands, who would let any man's spoken word stand between them and that husband's dead body. Should I ever marry, Watson, I should hope to inspire my wife with some feeling which would prevent her from being walked off by a housekeeper when my corpse was lying within a few yards of her."

Holmes to Watson,
The Valley of Fear, Part 1, Chap. 6

To Sherlock Holmes she is always *the* woman. I have seldom heard him mention her under any other name. In his eyes she eclipses and predominates the whole of her sex.

Watson on Irene Adler,
A Scandal in Bohemia

"She is the daintiest thing under a bonnet on this planet. So say the Serpentine-mews, to a man.

Holmes to Watson, on Irene Adler,
A Scandal in Bohemia

"Women are naturally secretive, and they like to do their own secreting."

Holmes to Watson,
A Scandal in Bohemia

"When a woman thinks that her house is on fire, her instinct is at once to rush to the thing which she values most. It is a perfectly overpowering impulse, and I have more than once taken advantage of it. In the case of the Darlington substitution scandal it was of use to me, and also in the Arnsworth Castle business. A married woman grabs at her baby; an unmarried one reaches for her jewel-box."

Holmes to Watson,
A Scandal in Bohemia

"What a woman – oh, what a woman!" cried the King of Bohemia, when we had all three read this epistle. "Did I not tell you how quick and resolute she was? Would she not have made an admirable queen? Is it not a pity that she was not on my level?"

"From what I have seen of the lady she seems indeed to be on a very different level to your Majesty," said Holmes coldly.

The King of Bohemia and Holmes,
A Scandal in Bohemia

And that was how a great scandal threatened to affect the kingdom of Bohemia, and how the best plans of Mr. Sherlock Holmes were beaten by a woman's wit. He used to make merry over the cleverness of women, but I have not heard him do it of late. And when he speaks of Irene Adler, or when he refers to her photograph, it is always under the honourable title of *the* woman.

Watson,
A Scandal in Bohemia

"Had there been women in the house, I should have suspected a mere vulgar intrigue."

Holmes to Watson,
The Red-Headed League

"I have seen too much not to know that the impression of a woman may be more valuable than the conclusion of an analytical reasoner."

Holmes to Mrs. Neville St. Clair,
The Man with the Twisted Lip

"There are women in whom the love of a lover extinguishes all other loves, and I think that she must have been one."

Holmes on Mary Holder,
The Beryl Coronet

In an experience of women which extends over many nations and three separate continents, I have never looked upon a face which gave a clearer promise of a refined and sensitive nature.

Watson on Mary Morstan,
The Sign of Four, Chap. 2

So we stood hand in hand like two children, and there was peace in our hearts for all the dark things that surrounded us.

Watson on Mary Morstan,
The Sign of Four, Chap. 5

"Women are never to be entirely trusted – not the best of them."

Holmes to Watson,
The Sign of Four, Chap. 7

I may have remarked before that Holmes had, when he liked, a peculiarly ingratiating way with women, and that he very readily established terms of confidence with them.

Watson on Holmes,
The Golden Pince-Nez

"Now, Watson, the fair sex is your department."

Holmes to Watson,
The Second Stain

Folk who were in grief came to my wife like birds to a lighthouse.

Watson on Mary Morstan,
The Man with the Twisted Lip

"And yet the motives of women are so inscrutable. ... How can you build on such a quicksand? Their most trivial action may mean volumes, or their most extraordinary conduct may depend upon a hairpin or a curling tongs."

Holmes to Watson,
The Second Stain

"Man or woman?" I asked.
"Oh, man, of course. No woman would ever send a reply-paid telegram. She would have come."

Watson and Holmes,
Wisteria Lodge

He had a remarkable gentleness and courtesy in his dealings with women. He disliked and distrusted the sex, but he was
always a chivalrous opponent.

Watson on Holmes,
The Dying Detective

"One of the most dangerous classes in the world," said he,
"is the drifting and friendless woman. She is the most harmless
and often the most useful of mortals, but she is the inevitable
inciter of crime in others. She is helpless. She is migratory. She
has sufficient means to take her from country to country and from
hotel to hotel. She is lost, as often as not, in a maze of obscure
pensions and boarding-houses. She is a stray chicken in a world
of foxes. When she is gobbled up she is hardly missed."

Holmes to Watson,
Lady Francis Carfax

"Women have seldom been an attraction to me, for my brain
has always governed my heart, but I could not look upon her
perfect clear-cut face, with all the soft freshness of the downlands
in her delicate colouring, without realizing that no young man
would cross her path unscathed."

Holmes on Maud Bellamy,
The Lion's Mane

"Who knows, Watson? Woman's heart and mind are insolu-
ble puzzles to the male."

Holmes to Watson,
The Illustrious Client

"Goodnight, Mister Sherlock Holmes."

Irene Adler to Holmes,
A Scandal in Bohemia

Sir Arthur Conan Doyle

Arthur Conan Doyle (1859-1930) was born in Edinburgh and received a Jesuit education at Stonyhurst College in Lancashire before returning to study medicine at Edinburgh University. It was one of his medical instructors, Dr. Joseph Bell, whose powers of observation and deduction later helped inspire Doyle's fictional detective, Sherlock Holmes.

Doyle practised medicine briefly in Southsea (after an even briefer stint on a whaling vessel, hence his knowledge of harpooning in *The Adventure of Black Peter*) before devoting his time increasingly to writing. He wrote more than 50 books — most famously the Sherlock Holmes stories, but also novels and short stories of adventure and science fiction, journalism and books of history, politics and religion. He was knighted in 1902, ostensibly for his historical account of the Boer War (in which he served as a medic), but also, some would say, for appeasing the reading public and resurrecting the supposedly dead Holmes in *The Hound of the Baskervilles* in 1901.

Oddly for the creator of the rational and logical Great Detective, Doyle devoted much of his later life to his strong beliefs in spiritualism and the existence of fairies, travelling the world and lecturing widely on the subject (including four trips to Canada). He was quick to denounce frauds and hucksters (of which there were many), but he seemed naïve and gullible in many respects. He became friends with the great magician and escape artist Harry Houdini, who likewise had a strong interest in spiritualism and in debunking frauds. But even though Houdini tried to persuade him otherwise, Doyle believed the performer had truly magical powers.

Conan Doyle had five children from two marriages, and it was largely his desperate attempts to connect with the spirit of the son from his first marriage, killed in the First World War, that fuelled his spiritualist beliefs. He died of heart failure in 1930, at the age of 71.

Index

The Sherlock Holmes Canon

A Study in Scarlet
The Sign of Four
The Hound of the Baskervilles
The Valley of Fear

Adventures of Sherlock Holmes
A Scandal in Bohemia
The Red-headed League
A Case of Identity
The Boscombe Valley Mystery
The Five Orange Pips
The Man with the Twisted Lip
The Adventure of the Blue Carbuncle
The Adventure of the Speckled Band
The Adventure of the Engineer's Thumb
The Adventure of the Noble Bachelor
The Adventure of the Beryl Coronet
The Adventure of the Copper Beeches

Memoirs of Sherlock Holmes
Silver Blaze
The Yellow Face
The Stock-broker's Clerk
The "Gloria Scott"
The Musgrave Ritual
The Reigate Puzzle
The Crooked Man
The Resident Patient
The Greek Interpreter
The Naval Treaty
The Final Problem

The Return of Sherlock Holmes
The Adventure of the Empty House
The Adventure of the Norwood Builder
The Adventure of the Dancing Men
The Adventure of the Solitary Cyclist
The Adventure of the Priory School

The Adventure of Black Peter
The Adventure of Charles Augustus Milverton
The Adventure of the Six Napoleons
The Adventure of the Three Students
The Adventure of the Golden Pince-Nez
The Adventure of the Missing Three-Quarter
The Adventure of the Abbey Grange
The Adventure of the Second Stain

His Last Bow
The Adventure of Wisteria Lodge
The Adventure of the Cardboard Box
The Adventure of the Red Circle
The Adventure of the Bruce-Partington Plans
The Adventure of the Dying Detective
The Disappearance of Lady Francis Carfax
The Adventure of the Devil's Foot
His Last Bow

The Case Book of Sherlock Holmes
The Adventure of the Illustrious Client
The Adventure of the Blanched Soldier
The Adventure of the Mazarin Stone
The Adventure of the Three Gables
The Adventure of the Sussex Vampire
The Adventure of the Three Garridebs
The Problem of Thor Bridge
The Adventure of the Creeping Man
The Adventure of the Lion's Mane
The Adventure of the Veiled Lodger
The Adventure of Shoscombe Old Place
The Adventure of the Retired Colourman

Quotable Sherlock
(from the works of Sir Arthur Conan Doyle)
© David W. Barber, 2001
All rights reserved

First published in Canada by
Quotable Books
an imprint of
Sound And Vision
359 Riverdale Avenue
Toronto, Canada M4J 1A4

http://www.soundandvision.com
E-mail: musicbooks@soundandvision.com
First edition, September 2001
1 3 5 7 9 11 13 15 - printings - 14 12 10 8 6 4 2

National Library of Canada
Cataloguing in Publication Data
Doyle, Arthur Conan, Sir, 1859-1930
Quotable Sherlock
(*Quotable Books*)
Includes bibliographical references and index
ISBN 0-920151-53-1
1. Holmes, Sherlock (Fictitious character)—
Quotations, maxims, etc
2. Doyle, Arthur Conan, Sir, 1859-1930—Quotations.
3. Quotations, English. I. Barber, David W.
(David William), 1958- II. Title. III. Series.
PR4623.A3 2001   823'.8   C2001-902002-3

Cover illustration by Kevin Reeves
Jacket design by Jim Stubbington
Typeset (of course) in Baskerville

Printed and bound in Canada

About the Editor

David W. Barber is a journalist and musician and the author of nine books of musical history and humor, including *Bach, Beethoven and the Boys, When the Fat Lady Sings,* and *Tutus, Tights and Tiptoes.* Formerly entertainment editor of the Kingston, Ont., *Whig-Standard* and editor of *Broadcast Week* magazine at the Toronto *Globe and Mail,* he's now a freelance journalist and musician in Toronto. As a composer, his works include two symphonies, a jazz mass based on the music of Dave Brubeck, a *Requiem,* several short choral and chamber works and various vocal-jazz songs and arrangements. He sings with the Toronto Chamber Choir and with his vocal-jazz group, Barber & the Sevilles, which has released a CD, called *Cybersex.*

By David W. Barber, cartoons by Dave Donald

A Musician's Dictionary
preface by Sir Yehudi Menuhin
isbn 0-920151-21-3

Bach, Beethoven and the Boys
Music History as it Ought to Be Taught
preface by Anthony Burgess
isbn 0-920151-10-8

When the Fat Lady Sings
Opera History as it Ought to Be Taught
preface by Maureen Forrester
foreword by Anna Russell
isbn 0-920151-34-5

If it Ain't Baroque
More Music History as it Ought to Be Taught
isbn 0-920151-15-9

Getting a Handel on Messiah
preface by Trevor Pinnock
isbn 0-920151-17-5

Tenors, Tantrums and Trills
An Opera Dictionary from Aida to Zzzz
isbn 0-920151-19-1

Tutus, Tights and Tiptoes
Ballet History as it Ought to Be Taught
preface by Karen Kain
isbn 0-920151-30-2

Other books from Sound And Vision and Quotable Books

Quotable Sherlock
by David W. Barber (Editor)
illustrations by Sidney Paget
isbn 0-920151-52-1

Quotable Alice
by David W. Barber (Editor)
illustrations by Sir John Tenniel
isbn 0-920151-52-3

Quotable Pop
Five Decades of Blah Blah Blah
by Phil Dellio & Scott Woods (Editor)
caricatures by Mike Rooth
isbn 0-920151-50-7

Quotable Opera
Aria ready for a Laugh?
by Steve Tanner (Editor)
illustrations by Umberto Tàccola
isbn 0-920151-54-X

Better Than It Sounds
A Dictionary of Humorous Musical Quotations
by David W. Barber (Editor)
isbn 0-920151-22-1

How to Stay Awake
During Anybody's Second Movement
by David E. Walden
cartoons by Mike Duncan
preface by Charlie Farquharson
isbn 0-920151-20-5

A Working Musician's Joke Book
by Daniel G. Theaker
cartoons by Mike Freen
preface by David W. Barber
isbn 0-920151-23-X

How To Listen To Modern Music
Without Earplugs
by David E. Walden
cartoons by Mike Duncan
foreword by Bramwell Tovey
isbn 0-920151-31-0

The Thing I've Played With the Most
Professor Anthon E. Darling Discusses
His Favourite Instrument
by David E. Walden
cartoons by Mike Duncan
foreword by Mabel May Squinnge, B.O.
isbn 0-920151-35-3

Opera Antics & Anecdotes
by Stephen Tanner
illustrations by Umberto Tàccola
foreword by David W. Barber
isbn 0-920151-31-0

I Wanna Be Sedated
Pop Music in the Seventies
by Phil Dellio & Scott Woods
caricatures by Dave Prothero
preface by Chuck Eddy
isbn 0-920151-16-7

The Composers
A Hystery of Music
by Kevin Reeves
preface by Daniel Taylor
isbn 0-920151-29-9

Love Lives of the Great Composers
From Gesualdo to Wagner
by Basil Howitt
isbn 0-920151-18-3

A Note from the Publisher

Sound And Vision is pleased to announce the creation of a new imprint called *Quotable Books*. The first three in the series are illustrated on the back cover. Other titles planned include *Quotable Shakespeare, Twain, Wilde, Poe, Blake, Dickens* and *Quotable Gumshoes*. The series will cover the arts, *Quotable Opera, Quotable Jazz,* and *Quotable Heavy Metal* plus literature and other subject areas, including politicians and statesmen such as Winston Churchill, Oliver Cromwell and Abraham Lincoln.

Our books may be purchased for educational or promotional use or for special sales. If you have any comments on this book or any other book we publish or if you would like a catalogue, please write to us at:

Sound And Vision,
359 Riverdale Avenue,
Toronto, Canada M4J 1A4.

Visit our Web site at: www.soundandvision.com. We would really like to hear from you.

We are always looking for suitable original books to publish. If you have an idea or manuscript, please contact us.

Thank you for purchasing or borrowing this book.

Geoffrey Savage
Publisher